Ken Lansdowne

The Art of Death

A Bent Mystery

7

H Publishing

Copyright © 2014 by Ken Lansdowne.

Publisher: H Publishing
    605 Clinton Street,
    Denver, Colorado 80247.

No part of this book may be reproduced in any form or by any means—including photocopying and electronic reproduction—without permission from the publisher.

PUBLISHERS NOTE: This is a work of fiction. Names, characters, and incidents are the product of the authors imagination or are used fictitiously. Any resemblance to actual persons living or dead, or events are entirely coincidental.

First Printing: 2014
Kindle: 2018

_ Library of Congress Cataloging in Publication Data
 The Art of Death : A Bent Mystery: a novel/ Ken Lansdowne
    p. cm.
  ISBN: 978-0-9740853-7-1
   1. Title

Printed in USA

H Publishing

BOOKS BY THE AUTHOR

Jacob Marley
A Gay Victorian Christmas Novella

THE BENT MYSTERY SERIES:
Secrets Don't Belong In Closets
A Murderous Ball Of Fluff
The Fairy Dust Killer
Home Sweet Homo
Dance:Ten Murder:Maybe?
A Mystery, Wrapped In A Mystery, Surrounded By A Mystery
The Art of Death
Bathhouse Bloodbath!

The Art of Death

Previously...

WHAT'S BEING PRESENTED here is what happened before the story I'm telling. A prequel, of sorts.

What I mean is that everything being told came before JB became involved in the case, but it definitely is a part of what happened after he did. This information was gleaned from sources other than the principals themselves, for obvious reasons you'll discover later. It arrives here far after the fact.

These events are placed here at the beginning simply so they may run in chronological order. They are here for sequential clarity only. They will eventually

The Art of Death 2

bring us to the main action of the story.

Are they necessary? You could live without it.

Are they important to the story? Very much.

What's here will give you a far clearer understanding of what will come later.

You also need to be aware that what is being told here is hearsay at best. You know what is said about hearsay? There's the story of the person who did it, the person who saw it, and the person who heard about it. What follows is mostly the latter. Perhaps it is the truth. Who can say? Just know that it is filtered through the eyes of those who were stationed on the outer perimeters of the action.

The reason behind this further investigation came from John Weatherwax's family arriving in New York City to retrieve his belongings. His mother wanted an explanation for what had happened to her son. Completely understandable, given the circumstances. She insisted that what had happened, according to the "Christian" way John had been raised, was completely out of character for him. She wanted to know why. She needed a reason to explain it before she could have any sense of closure. The police, however, were unwilling to help her — after all they had plenty of other cases they were working by then. John's case was already closed. Finished. Done. Moldering in dusty files.

Mostly to get the woman out of his thinning hair NYPD Lieutenant Martin Greenberg, who had handled the case initially, directed her to JB — that would be Jeremy Bent to those who might have read one of his mystery novels. He's called JB by his more intimate acquaintances.

He'd had some dealings with the case as you will see, and after meeting with the mother he agreed to take on the task of filling in some of the blanks for her. Who could refuse a grieving mother, right? A secondary reason was that JB wanted to satisfy his own curiosity about the entire string of events. He liked his cases tied up in ribbons all neat and pretty. He wanted to understand why Death had decided to take its toll on these particular participants?

While helping the mother to pack his apartment JB found John Weather wax's day planner and address book. It was the standard item; black leatherette covers with gold embossed lettering for the year 1987. These handy booklets can be found in almost any stationery store, especially in November and December before the upcoming year. John's planner had pages for the day and date of the month. Each day on a separate page with lines below to list any appointments.

Instead John had used these lines as a kind of truncated journal or diary; putting notes down to record the events of that day. Did the laundry, picked up dog food, twenty dollars into savings that sort of thing. The planner covered the previous few months, and became the basis for JB's entire investigation. It was in these hand-written notes scribbled next to each date along with phone interviews with the people whose addresses and numbers were listed that JB found the threads to weave a story.

It gave him the following:

April 19, 1987: *Met R.H. today. A stone cold fox! Hunka. Hunka! Just my type. We exchanged numbers. Maybe he'll call?*

R.H. would have to be Robin. He was a young man on the move. Maybe not upward, probably only sideways, but definably going somewhere. He was also a consummate user and con man. If John Weatherwax had been privy to that single piece of information none of what follows would have happened. They had met on a sunny Sunday at a brunch given by a friend of John's at his beachfront apartment in Venice, California.

John Weatherwax himself was a thirty year old gay man who worked as the manager of the J. Paul Getty Museum gift shop over in Malibu. It was an okay job that allowed John to pursue his hobby: the collecting of West Coast regional art. His collection wasn't much to write home about yet, a couple of good landscapes, and an early Hockney drawing with gouache he had lucked upon on a visit to a local thrift store.

Weatherwax was a single man; forty pounds overweight, wore bottle thick glasses, had bad skin, and yearned for someone to love. It would prove to be his greatest weakness. So far his love extended only to a rescue dog he'd found the year before. A good natured little animal who was so ugly she was adorable. He called her Sweets. It was short for Sweetdarlingcutiepie.

Robin, mentioned before, was in his mid twenties. He was blond, had shocking blue eyes, and a ready smile (if it wasn't just a little too adroit). He was handsome without being ravishing and a Hustler. Note the capital H. What he didn't have in looks he made up for with a kind of oozy charisma. He could charm many most of the time, to paraphrase Mr. Lincoln.

He was at brunch that Sunday in Venice trying to finagle one of the other guests to come in with him on a deal he had in mind. Robin always was working some sort of deal. It should be made clear that the term Hustler as applied to Robin doesn't mean that he was a male prostitute, available to gay men for a price. In truth, he was straight, or rather a tiny bit bisexual, and a Hustler only in the most entrepreneurial sense of the word. He'd always felt that gay money was just as spendable as anybody else's money. He was very liberal that way. He also believed that gay men had large disposable incomes that they might invest in one of his schemes. That was enough for him. He and John Weatherwax were a train wreck charging toward each other at full speed.

Robin was working to get enough money to back an illegal con he was planning. He had ended up following a grifter's career path as the result of an innate laziness on his part. It prevented him from looking for more legitimate work. Dirty fingernails and sweaty brows were not for him. Coupled with his growing up in the New Jersey State Foster Care System from the age of six he was destined for the shadier side of life. Cons and scams were simply a survival tactic for him. The foster system had thrown him hither and thither, from home to home, and left him with few usable abilities to survive with. He was, however, able to pick up new skills easily, a very important attribute when hustling your way through life. Early on he had been in Times Square in New York City and watched as two kids took a crowd of suckers with their sleight of hand card game. Hours later, on another street corner, Robin was running his own Three-card Monte game. And winning.

That was when he was fifteen. He'd run away that year from the last place New Jersey had stuck him. An abusive household that considered him merely a meal ticket and slave to the old lady that ran the house. He'd left a bag of dog shit on fire in the kitchen one late night, and left.

Eventually he ran all the way out to California, where he felt he might get by. He landed in Los Angeles in mid-November of Nineteen eighty-three. It was sunny and cozy, not at all like the snowy cold East Coast environs he'd been used to. Plus he found the whole town to be one giant hustle, full of citizens on the make. He fit right in.

April 24, 1987: *R called me! Having dinner tonight. Said he wants to ask about something. I wonder what?*

Later: Dinner over. R is great. We talked about art. And his need for cash from some pieces he has. He offered an unusual opportunity. May take him up on it. I do have some misgivings though...

Robin found himself in a particularly unique position to get the drawings he needed for the latest gambit he was working. It was a basic "fake and bake" con but he hadn't worked out the last part of it yet. He needed some sort of twist at the end.

He was at that moment living in the home of a once famous actress named Blossom Skyler. She had been around Hollywood since the Forties and played flighty housewives and dithering dowagers in countless B-movies for RKO, Columbia and Republic studios.

Then she had hit it big in the early days of television with a comedy series custom fit to her scatterbrained character. *Springtime For Sissy* had run for nine full seasons, and had won her several Emmys and Photoplay awards. The series also served to introduce her to the executive producer of the sitcom. One Hermie Slotkin.

Hermie became her last husband. That was husband number five for Blossom. She was number three for Hermie. After they married he went on to produce and create a bevy of hit TV programs in that golden age. *West The Wagons* and *Hollywood Hills Cop* were his. As was *The Harvey Hoard*, now considered a classic of the genre.

They had lived richly and lavishly in a thirty-five room Beverly Hills mansion that Blossom was still living in when Robin came into her life thirty years later. The house wasn't quite so lavish anymore. In actuality it was more mausoleum than showplace by then. Hermie had died several years before and Blossom had become mostly a recluse. A loyal maid and a handyman were her only staff, as the more flighty aspects of her scattered personality had taken her off into a world of her own design. She had become much like the fictional Norma Desmond of *Sunset Boulevard* movie fame. Robin had been sent to her home in his capacity as PA (personal assistant) to Rowdy Frankel, the actor. Robin was at Blossom's house to deliver a script. They wanted the old broad to play Rowdy's grandmother for a six episode arc on his TV series, *The Wellington's*. Soap Operas were big that season.

Robin had managed to wheedle his way into the PA position by pulling an, even for him, meanspirited little con. He'd gotten his predecessor caught up in a robbery charge. It had been easy enough to implicate the schmuck by leaving his wallet at the scene of the theft Robin himself had committed. Robin had lifted the guy's wallet at a bar the night before. There was nothing that Robin wouldn't stoop to when he wanted something. Theft, lies, forgery — all and or any of them. It didn't matter. If it got him what he wanted it was on the table.

So, the script he was delivering to the ramshackle mansion was easily tossed aside when Blossom, upon laying her demented eyes on him, made a huge fuss over him. Although confused by her ravings, why would Robin stop her? Of course he'd wait and see what it was about.

It turned out Blossom had mistaken Robin for her son, Arnie. He decided right off not to disabuse her of her belief, even if he knew her son had been killed in the Korean Conflict. What? Twenty years earlier? But if Blossom wanted to treat him as if he was her long lost kid. What the hell? He had moved into the mansion within the week.

Dr. Janet Snyder:

(310)555-0345-W (323)555-8765-H
John Weather wax's immediate supervisor at the Getty Museum in a phone call.

"I don't know what I can tell you? John was excellent at his job here at the villa. We were very sorry to lose him. But he saw an opportunity for advancement and, rightfully, he grabbed it. I can't blame him for that. He took a position in New York City I believe. We would have appreciated his giving us some notice, but that wasn't possible as he needed to report for the job immediately. At least that was how he explained it to me. You see John and I were friends and work colleagues both. We dined together quite often. So it came as quite a surprise when he told me what was happening. In my personal view, I believe it had something to do with his affair with that Robin boy. Poor John was absolutely besotted by him. I was fully aware of John's sexual orientation, and it had no affect on his position here, or on our relationship for that matter. But Robin seemed to have no other means of support than John, so I was, I must admit, distrustful of his intentions toward my friend. I found out Robin's status when it was explained that he was the primary reason for John's moving out of California so quickly. Robin had been thrown out of his current living arrangement and threatened to leave John if he didn't move back East for this job he was being offered. As I said, Robin did seem to hold John in a Svengali like thrall. It turned out the person who was purchasing a piece from John's personal art collection was the person who had offered him the position in New York. Presumably, he was someone very important in the corporation John would be working for..."

A telegram was tucked between the day planner pages of the month of April. Dated 4/9/87 and sent by Edward Weatherwax to his son John.
John
Decision unfathomable. Are you sane? Life is ruined. Seek help.
Dad

Exactly ten words. The very words that every gay man or woman dreads hearing from their parent. John's father was objecting to his son's life choice and finding it needful of "help". What sort of help could only be imagined. Therapy? Castration? Lobotomy? All are legally still on the table for gay men even in today's supposedly enlightened age. It is the reason so many gay people will stay closeted. That familial disapproval shattering relationships, tearing apart households, rending us adrift and alone.

It also had to be a mitigating factor in John's decision to go to New York with Robin. To become a partner in the scam Robin was perpetrating. Without his family as rudder John must have latched onto Robin as a life preserver, not realizing Robin was even more of a shipwreck then he was.

April 27, 1987: *...need to find art student. Then will need to look for a buyer.*

It had been easy enough for Robin to wander around the mansion and check out what goodies the crazy old lady owned. With thirty-five rooms and one tenant there were rooms in the house that hadn't been visited in decades. In the closed off left wing, at the end of a long hall, Robin found a storage room filled with stacked and abandoned boxes. He knew he'd been right about no one knowing what might be in them from the dusty undisturbed condition they were in. Opening one and flipping through the contents, he found photo albums filled with eight by ten glossys of old time movie stars. Clark Gable. Spencer Tracy. Madeleine Carroll. And a bunch of other stars he didn't know. All of them were signed to Blossom and her husband. Other boxes held bound movie scripts, press books, lobby card sets, folded posters, things of that sort. All of it, within a week or two had been delivered to *MovieTone News*, a memorabilia and collectors store down on Sunset. Robin was making as much as forty bucks for some of the photos alone.

Another room yielded an impressive stack of framed paintings and drawings. They looked to him like they could be worth something. Unfortunately, Robin's knowledge of fine art was minimal at best. A visit to the Beverly Hills public library gave him a quickly learned yeoman's understanding of what was good and what wasn't. It was in that studying of art books that the beginnings of the scam were worked out in Robin's feverish brain.

His thinking ran thusly: if you just sell a painting you have the money that one time only. But if you sell it more than once you have the same money multiple times. Isn't many better than once? Question: How could he sell the same work more than once? Answer: You sell a copy. Question: But who would pay big bucks for a copy? Which led directly to the answer: They would pay it if they *didn't* know it was a copy. If they *thought* they had the original.

Now the question became how was he going to make that happen? That's where he was stumped. The details. He'd have to think about it some. Meanwhile, what could he get for, say, that little drawing of a clown dancing with a rabbit playing a violin he'd seen in Blossom's storeroom? Signed by some fruity art guy named Chagall? What was it worth, he wondered?

Robin had talked to a guy that Sunday before,

at brunch, who seemed to know a lot about art and painting and shit. Maybe Robin could get together with him and find out what he needed to know? What the hell was his name? Weather something. He had given Robin his number. He'd call.

April 29, 1987: *Found student in museum art classes. Will make copies for $100 each. Cheap at half that.*

Robin had been able to carry the Chagall drawing out of the old lady's house right under her nose. No problem. Frame and all. He'd just wrapped it in an old blanket. Hell, she didn't even ask him what it was he had as he walked by. She waved merrily as he slipped the drawing in the car and drove off. Not even caring that he was carrying off an art work worth a shitload of money. After getting together with John Weatherwax and finding out that little scribble was worth thousands of dollars it was a done deal.

It was John; during the dinner they'd had together, who had come up with the finer points of a workable scam with Robin. It turned out John had a knack for figuring out these things. His was a logical mind in action. Combining all the elements Robin had been thinking about, then adding the final twist he needed. As they talked into the night they had figured it all out. First, they needed to get some artist, a student at one of the local art academies maybe, to make a copy of the drawing for them. Then they would switch the copy with the original at the right time. After the mark had paid.

Robin had known right off he had John in the palm of his hand. He knew John was crazy about him. Queers always fell for him, so this guy wanting him didn't surprise him. He'd used gay men as his suckers before. He wasn't that way himself, but he wasn't averse to letting them want him when it suited his purposes.

When Robin got the Chagall drawing to John's place they found they had a bonus. When they took it out of its frame, they found another drawing by some other artist was behind it. Some guy named Miro signed this one. It was only a few lines and some shapes, but John said it was worth as much as the rabbit picture. Art is funny that way. So they had the copy guy make them one of each. Robin figured it was double the scam, double the cash.

May 2, 1987: *Buddy called. Invited me to dinner with some New York friend of his who's here to visit my museum.*

John went to that dinner that night never expecting it to become the opportunity it turned out to be. The guest was a man named Bevan Jones, who was a wealthy art collector from back East. He wanted to see the Getty. The museum was still new enough that art connoisseurs were coming from all over to tour it. John was supposed to give him an insiders view. Bevan and John hit it off right away. With their mutual interests it wasn't any big surprise.

John even took advantage of that interest to introduce the idea that he was in the market to sell a piece from his own collection. A fine little Chagall drawing. As a reason he cited a need for money because of a family emergency. John had been almost shocked at how trippingly the lies had fallen from his tongue. How easy it was to reel this Jones fellow into the trap he and Robin were setting for him.

Buddy Sharp:
(310)555-3457(H)
One of John's friends in a phone call.

"I had no idea what was going on, although I myself, along with all of John's other friends I might add, were utterly mystified by his relations with that Robin slag. What a piece of shit he was. It was all so horribly tacky. Robin was pretty enough, fer shur, but such an obvious sleazeball. Grody to the max."

JB was always surprised and delighted by the twists and diphthongs that the English language managed to take. But it did distress him that a fifteen year old Valley

Girl was needed to translate the current vernacular.

"...but John just wouldn't see it. He was in love. We all warned him that it wasn't going to turn out good for him. None of us had any idea how awful it was really going to be.

I had asked him to dinner that night in the hopes he and Bevan would hit it off. Bevan was simply perfect for John. He's got money. He collects art like John. He owns several business ventures. He was a real catch. I admit I was playing matchmaker. They just had so much in common. It seemed so perfect. They did end up getting along like gangbusters, but only in a business like way. Bevan even offered John a job as executive manager of his bookstore in New York City. That was a few days later. Right after that Robin moved in with John, I think. I certainly didn't approve of that, but John said he'd been thrown out of the house he'd been staying in because the old lady that owned the place was a wacko. I'll bet she caught him doing something dishonest and kicked his ass to the curb. That's what I think.

Anyway, John was living in a tiny one-bedroom apartment. There wasn't enough room for the two of them at his place When Bevan offered him that job it seemed like a perfect way to take care of the situation. I was told that Robin sorta forced it on John. That John didn't really want to leave, but he did what Robin wanted. Love often makes one do really stupid things..."

May 27, 1987: *In New York City? Can't believe it. It all happened so fast. Bevan offered to take the drawing. Then turned around and offered me a job as manager of his store! Robin wanted to leave Calif. anyway, so I agreed. And here we are!*

It had been a whirlwind for those last couple of weeks. First Bevan Jones had taken John up on his offer to buy the Chagall drawing. The deal would happen after Bevan had the piece authenticated. Since the drawing was the real thing John had no objection to that. Then Bevan had taken him completely by surprise, and offered him a terrific job as manager of his bookstore. In New York. At way more money than John was currently making. And he could bring Robin along. Bevan said he would even pay for the move.

Robin was originally from back East so he was excited by the prospect of going back and pushed John to accept the position. In reality Robin was feeling the hot breath of another John on his neck. John Law. The old lady had found out about his nefarious dealings with her personal property and turned him in. She wanted him charged with larceny and grand theft. He needed to get out of town. Fast.

They had packed, called the moving company, and flown to New York, all in two days. They stayed at one of Bevan's corporate apartments for a few days, and then John found a sweet little place on the Upper West Side. Small, not much money, and in a good neighborhood. There was even another smaller studio right upstairs for Robin to stay in. They both moved in. The little apartment came furnished so John was settled quickly once the moving van arrived with his belongings.

The only major mishap was during the move a bottle of liquid had spilled and spoiled the all important copies of both the Chagall and the Miro drawings. They were ruined. Totally unusable.

They thought for a moment of halting the scam with Bevan, but then Robin admitted he knew of someone who could do two new copies for them. He only had to locate him. Someone from his past was all Robin told John. So John delayed giving the Chagall to Bevan for the authentication process, which gave time for Robin to find this new artist.

May 30, 1987: *It's fate I tell you. My first day at work and I meet a man who wants to buy the* Miro. *Unbelievable. This whole thing is going to work out.*

John was reshelving the art books after his lunch break when a customer looking over the volumes started talking with him. The man turned out to be a collector who was interested in what John had to offer. Especially when John mentioned the low price he wanted for it. Again the lies rolled out like goo on a goose feather. John had convinced the man it was a legitimate deal easily, but it was really the mark's own avarice and greed that sold the thing. That was the very nature of a con Robin had taught him. It was all a kind of theatre of the absurd and they, the con men, were the puppeteers. They, through feeding the mark what they wanted, controlled them and made them jig to the tune they were playing. The marks pay for their piggishness and greed by giving up their money.

Of course, the man wanted to get the drawing vetted. Not a problem John assured him. We can meet and you may take the drawing to anybody you choose for the purpose. Appointments were set.

Now they had no choice but to get those copies.

June 22, 1987: *The deal is in motion. Having the* Miro *vetted overnight and the mark will pay when it is certified as original. Will take $500.00 on the initial deal.*

Robin managed to come up with a very good copy of the Miro in short order. He said his artist guy was working on the Chagall, and would have it ready before the week was out. Having the copy in hand led John to meet his bookstore mark with the original drawing. Together they walked the drawing to a Madison Avenue gallery so it could be checked out. The guy had fallen for the story John had told him completely. A heart wrenching tale concerning operations and relatives and hospital bills worked every time, according to Robin, who knew about these things.

After getting the authentication the mark even invited John to come back to his Park Avenue apartment to see him hang the signed Miro drawing in his den. That gave John a chance to case the place and memorize the layout so Robin could come back later with the purpose of stealing the original drawing. That was the twist. By stealing the original they could easily replace it with a copy, and the mark would be so glad to have it back he wouldn't even notice the switch.

It had been easy enough to put a signature on their copy. All it took was a facsimile of the artist's real signature and a light box. John had ever so carefully traced the artists name onto the forgery with black India ink and a calligraphy brush he'd bought at an art supply store.

Later that night, Robin, dressed all in black, with a ridiculous Mexican wrestlers mask he'd bought that afternoon over his face, went to the mark's apartment. He broke in with a crowbar through the back kitchen entrance. He'd said that security people always tended to put less than top of the line alarms on back doors since maids and such were in and out so often. He grabbed the drawing, and a couple of other items to make it look like a real robbery, and was out of the place within ten minutes. The mark wasn't even home; he was out celebrating the great deal he had wrangled for the drawing.

The next morning Robin called the mark, disguised his voice, and demanded eight thousand dollars for the return of the items he'd taken, including the Miro. The mark didn't even report it to the police. He paid that same afternoon by leaving the cash in a telephone booth which John picked up when he could see the coast was clear. Robin left the rolled up Miro forgery on a bench in Central Park. It was a perfect con. A sterling fake and bake. The fake was the Miro. The baked was the mark, out several thousand for a forged drawing.

John had to admit he was hooked on the excitement of the whole gambit. What he didn't admit were the doubts nipping at his conscience. Robin was eager to start working the second scam, with the Chagall.

July 20, 1987: *R is really pissed at me. I never saw him so mad. Might be trouble.*

John had been having increasing guilt pangs about what they were doing. Guilt over what thieves they had become. It didn't set well with that hard-shell Baptist upbringing of his. All that talk of damnation and hell fire as a kid had its effect. He wanted to stop.

It came to a head when he told Robin that he didn't want to go through with the Chagall scam. They had already given the drawing to Bevan Jones at that point. He was in the process of having it authenticated. John wanted to let it go at that. Essentially sell the drawing for the money they had asked for and leave it. Finish it. Fini.

Robin couldn't believe it. The real money didn't come until the mark paid the ransom. What was John thinking?

What he was thinking was that the job with Bevan had turned out to be a really good one. Way better than he had expected and one that John liked. He was making a good honest living, with bonuses and perks. Making more than enough to have a comfortable life in the city. Why should he screw it up by stealing from the man that paid his salary? Even if Bevan didn't tip to the fake, it didn't seem right to scam his boss this way.

Robin was dumbfounded. And angry. He could only see that a crapload of money was slipping through his fingers. And that wasn't going to happen. He raged, he cajoled, he schmoozed, he questioned. He used all his charms to get John to keep on with the deal. Hours they were at it. Robin wouldn't let it go. John wouldn't give in. John refused to hear it. John even went so far as to say he would call the cops on them. On himself, for Christ's sake. Robin didn't give a rat's furry ass that confession was good for the soul. It was his own ass that he was worried about.

Finally, John, in frustration, let drop that Bevan had sent the drawing to a shop for framing. Robin snapped to a bigger truth. He didn't need John to do the con. He could run the scam all by himself, without John's whining and shit. Why not? He'd get the ransom money and dump him. Lose the fool. It was a plan.

❊❊❊

And that was it. All the content of the day planner that was relevant. John, it turned out, knew too much and had crossed the wrong person. So grim Death had pushed the starter button and began the wheels to turning...

Chapter 1

BETTY BUCKLEY FINISHED her set on a high note with what had to be the thousandth rendition of *Memory* she had sung since her opening night in *CATS* years before. She was stuck with the song like Liza was with *Cabaret* or Elaine Stritch with *The Ladies Who Lunch*. She took her bow to appreciative applause from the crowd, then Marion Seldes came back as the mistress of ceremonies and started to introduce the next act.

She was graciously hosting one more AIDS benefit. Lately these benefits were being held as often as gay bears have anonymous sex in the Central Park brambles. This benefit, on a muggy evening in July, was being held for ACT-UP, which was a new activist group, started only a few months before, to protest, among other causes, the high cost of AZT. AZT was the first medication that had been developed that showed any real promise in the treatment of AIDS. The drug company, however, was greedily gouging patients for what was the only medicine available. The company was charging as much as ten thousand dollars a year per patient for a medicine that cost less than a dollar to manufacture. It was outrageous.

JB hadn't been aware of this pharmaceutical rip-off until Len Matthews — yes, that would be the actor and Broadway star, and incidentally JB's best friend — had pointed it out to him. Len had been attending meetings of the new group being feted that evening, and was becoming quite the gay militant of late. In fact, Len was the reason for JB's attendance at the benefit to begin with. He was appearing that evening with Lee Arden, the costar of his current Broadway show. They were voluntarily appearing to sing the duet they did eight times a week for the benefit crowd. Len had provided JB a ticket and warned him not to be late. It wasn't as if JB had such a busy social life anyway. His day planner had been blank for the evening and being entertained by a gaggle of glitteringly famous people wasn't such an arduous task at that.

Another of the rewards of attending these benefits was having a chance for what was lately being called "networking" among the stock exchange Yuppie types down on Wall Street. The Broadway community tended to overlap with the gay community in New York, so attending most any gay event was a good way to catch up with the other. JB also had a minor reputation within the theatre community as a playwright and play doctor, and it never hurt to get the latest talk from one or another of his connected and gossipy acquaintances. Sometimes a job lead could come from a simple chance encounter. He had run into several of his friends already, including Dalton Hughes, the director of JB's last play. They had exchanged pleasantries and left it at that, since neither of them had any projects that might interest the other at the moment.

But at the intermission here was Dalton again bearing down on JB with a young lady in tow. What the hell did he want now?

The young woman Dalton had by the arm was, even to JB's jaded New Yorker eyes, a classic beauty of the Hollywood variety. Project this girl on a forty foot movie screen and most any group of straight men would end up looking like a pack of dogs being shown a card trick. She was a champagne blond in a tight low cut designer cocktail gown, radiating what is called in the biz "star quality". She definitely was from the West Coast, JB surmised, her look was far to light and natural to be from New York's more sooty environs.

As they got closer JB finally recognized her. Her name was Starzy Hillard, obviously not her real name by the stretch of anyone's imagination, except perhaps an overly quixotic publicity agent. She was one of the hot talents being touted by the Hollywood movie industry. She had been appearing in a long line of increasingly vapid rom-coms, that's what romantic comedies were called by the trade, which had been seeing decreasing revenues of late. That was according to the trade papers JB read every morning.

She was simply the latest in a long line that had started with Jean Harlow, segued into Betty Grable, was surpassed by Marilyn Monroe, continued with Joey Heatherton the generation before this one, and now had Starzy vying for the title of this year's Sex Goddess. Why Dalton was hauling her toward JB wasn't clear, but JB girded loin for the confrontation nonetheless.

She didn't meet his expectations at all. JB had expected another Hollywood bimbette of legend and lore. You know the type, dumb-ish and available to go down on bended nylon at a moments notice. Instead she was articulate, intelligent, and quite charming in a spacey actressey sort of way. Nothing JB wasn't used to after hanging around with Len Matthews for the years they'd been friends.

Dalton made his introduction and then slid away to leave them together. A few minutes of conversation made for initial impressions, then, after an awkward pause, Starzy got directly to her reason for wanting to meet JB. She had cajoled Dalton into introducing her so that she could talk with him about a business deal she had in mind.

"You want to what?" JB scratched at the back of his head.

"My production company would like to option the movie rights to one of your books," she answered. "Is that so unusual?" It was becoming less unusual lately as more and more performers were taking charge of their own careers and generating their own projects instead of waiting for a studio to do it. What was that line about inmates running the asylum?

"Well, it doesn't happen every day around here."

"It does where I come from. What I have in mind is a six month option to explore the possibly of turning the novel into a suitable movie script."

"Which book are we talking about?"

"Your second.*** I'd love to play the female lead."

JB gaped. "You're joking? Are you sure you read the book?"

Since JB's second book had only one female the correct age among its characters he was somewhat taken aback by her desire to play her. The plot concerned transforming said female from an ugly duckling into a better looking duck. How could this ravishing creature even begin to think she was right for such a part?

"Of course I've read it. Several times. It's the kind of serious part I've been looking for. Something other

---

***That would be *A Murderous Ball of Fluff*, Number 2 in the Bent Mystery series.

than the sex doll that my last few pictures have made me out to be."

"I'm flattered you're interested, of course, but I just don't see it, Ms. Hillard. Maybe you should look elsewhere for your serious part? I don't think the character in my book could be changed enough to accommodate your persona."

"Please, don't be so quick about it. Could we meet tomorrow for lunch? Then we could discuss it further..."

"I'd be happy to meet with you. I never turn down a free lunch. You did say you were buying, didn't you?" JB didn't pause for her to answer. "But I really don't see how it can work. You are far too beautiful to play the woman described in my book."

She crossed her arms over her ample cleavage. "You have something I want, Mr. Bent. I would like to discuss terms." JB could see the shadows of a very savvy businesswoman under all the sex goddess make-up and clothes she had on. He realized he shouldn't underestimate her.

"Call me JB. Everybody does. But I don't see what you could possibly say that..." That's when Ms. Seldes started introducing Len and Lee. "I'm sorry, but these are my friends. I have to watch them. We'll meet tomorrow then?"

She nodded as JB's attention was drawn to the front of the room.

Len and Lee were greeted with much applause. Both were still wearing their respective Eighteen-ninety's costumes from their show, apparently having just left the stage and come straight to the benefit.

Len spoke quickly to the piano player and then stepped up to the microphone. "Thank you very much. Let's get right into this, okay?" There was more applause. He pulled at the handlebar mustache he had pasted under his lip for the part he played. Once it was off he made a comedy bit out of not knowing what to do with it. He looked around, saw there was no one to help, so took the mustache and put it on his forehead. He suddenly had very bushy eyebrows. And got a laugh out of it. Smiling, he said, "I don't get a chance to sing a ballad very often, so I'd like to do that now. This is one of Jerry Herman's most lovely ones..." and the first notes of *If He Walked Into My Life* from the show *Mame* were played.

Len removed the comic eyebrow and sang the song in a strong serious voice, giving it the same depth of feeling and lament that Eydie Gorme had used for her pop version, and took the audience by surprise by not changing the lyric. He left the gender of the song as it was originally written. No shes for the hes, no hers for the hims. Len knew his audience, that was plainly evident. He even got some scattered applause in the middle of the song for doing it his way.

Next Lee Arden stepped up and had her turn at the mic. She continued the musical gender bending by singing the title song from the show *She Loves Me,* again not changing those pesky pronouns.

Then, for their duet, they stepped back into their current stage roles. Lee said, "I guess that'll be enough of the gay lyrics for tonight."

Feigning surprise with a huge double take, Len said, "You mean what we just sang was gay?"

"About as gay as a tangerine...or a French horn."

"Funny, I never thought of a French horn as being all that gay. Now a piccolo...that's a different story." They got their expected laugh.

The piano player started the introduction to their song. The two sang the duet from their show with gusto and to loud applause.

And with the song's last note the entertainment portion of the evening was over. Ms. Seldes came back and said the appropriate things to wind it down, telling the audience to leave their checks, it was a benefit after all, at the front desk.

Chapter 2

A FEW HOURS later JB heard a knock on his apartment door. It was after one AM. Who the hell?

It had to be Len. He and Len were probably the only two people in the building who would still be awake at that hour. Len because his normal work day in the theater always ended after eleven PM, and JB because he had been having some trouble sleeping of late. He would lay down, sleep for an hour, and then be awake again until five or so in the morning. It was irritating in that there wasn't any real reason for it. Just an underlying sense that something was amiss. A sense of discontent JB couldn't explain away. It wasn't a full out depression, just a sense of malaise.

JB checked the peephole to find it was who he expected. He opened the door and Len, hunched over and dragging a foot behind him, entered, crying out, "Sanctuary. Sanctuary." He was doing a so-so impression of Charles Laughton as the Hunchback of Paris. Or was it Boris Karloff?

"You do know how to make an entrance, I must say. What's this about?"

"I need protection, good sir..." It was Karloff. "The gendarme may be on my heels as I speak. Knocking upon your door to carry me off to the Bastille..."

"Cut it out, Len. What are you going on about?"

He stood up straight, leaving Karloff behind. "I've broken the law, JB. That's what I've done. I knew it was wrong, but I had to have it. You don't pass up a chance like this. It's..."

"Now I'm getting worried. What the hell have you done?"

While they were talking Len had walked through the kitchen and into JB's office. He was now coming back with a couple of push pins in his hand. He unbuttoned his summer weight overcoat and from its folds he pulled out a long roll of paper he had stored under his armpit.

"It was this, JB. I was in the subway on my way home tonight and this was up at Grand Central. I saw it and had to grab it."

He unrolled the paper and pinned it to a blank expanse of wall by JB's kitchen door.

"Oh, my Lord." JB said with complete awe in his voice. He grabbed Len's arm. "I can totally understand the impulse."

When the NYC subway system had unpaid advertising spaces along its twenty-six lines and four-hundred and sixty-eight stations they would paste a black sheet of matte paper over the space to cover the expired broadside that was already there. These huge thirty-two by seventy-eight inch rectangles were a perfect canvas for various graffiti artists to showcase their work. Keith Haring, for one, had started his art career using these spaces for exactly that purpose. The drawings of his electric babies and cartoon like chalk figures had begun appearing in the subways as early as Nineteen-eighty. Now that Haring had become so famous others were following in his footsteps by using these black spaces to showcase their own work. There were probably three different artists at work currently. But only one of them had managed to push his way to the forefront and become a sought after star of the artistic cliques in the city.

He signed his work Jathan, but no one really knew who that was. So far.

JB, cynic that he could be, knew that when a prestigious gallery show was offered Jathan would come out from the shadows into the glare of the public light. Until then he was this mysterious figure who was said to draw his pieces while wearing a mask, and who did his drawings late at night when no one was around the tunnels of the system. That way the rush hour morning commuters would be treated to the sight of these beautiful fragile works as they made their way to work in the midst of all the power and violence that the subways entailed. The public was enthralled with him and his work.

His drawings were very different from Haring's in that he drew with a more illustratrative eye. Where Haring used white chalk only, Jathan used pastels and bursts of color. Where Haring drew his basic simplistic line cartoons, Jathan drew more realistically. There was also a razor sharp satirical edge to his work, much like the English broadsides of nineteenth century England. His recent skewing of Ed Koch over his "friend" — read lady beard for the gay and deeply closeted New York City mayor — Bess Meyerson's patronage scandal had even managed to bring Jathan some national attention.

His drawing had Koch frantically holding his closet door closed while Bess was just as frantically banging her fists on the other side. The caption had read "You can't come in. There's only room for one person to hide in this closet."

"How did you get it?" JB asked, referring to Len's find.

"I saw it there in Grand Central Station, took out my trusty Swiss Army knife, and cut away. There's got to be at least four other layers behind this. But isn't it terrific?"

"I'll say."

The drawing was of a merman, a half fish and half hunk. It was Jathan's male figure drawings that were the most sought after of all his works. By the gay intelligentsia at least. Obviously influenced by the likes of Tom of Finland and other gay erotic illustrators, Jathan's men were all stunning in their rough hewn masculine beauty. Square of jaw, possessing deep soulful eyes, all were well muscled and mightily endowed. They were simply gorgeous.

"Isn't it beautiful..." Len heaved a sigh. "...if only I could find the model."

"Yeah, that type could walk by a package of dough and make instant Mint Milano cookies. I bet I could even sleep after a session with that hunk."

"You're still having trouble sleeping?"

"Yep. I don't know what it is. Anxiety. Worry. Some odd concern. Something's getting at me."

"Maybe you need something to do. A hobby? You could take up knitting? A project to occupy your convoluted and devious little mind."

"No, about the only do it yourself project I can handle right now is self-pity."

"How about a new case to play Miss Marple with? I bet that would perk you right up."

"You have anything in mind? Anyone you know been knocked off lately?"

"Read the papers. There's always some maniac loose or some dastardly crime wave in the making in the *Post*."

"You mean like a thief that cuts drawings out of the subways?"

"Is that really a crime or simply art appreciation?"

JB regarded the drawing. "You know what I really can appreciate is the acceptance this Jathan is getting from the main line art establishment. Most gay artists get neutered or hetro-sexualized right off the bat. There is no homoerotic work allowed. You know I read one of Andy Warhol's obituaries back in February and the fact he was gay wasn't even mentioned. Can you believe it? As a writer I know how my being gay affects my work. As a visual artist it had to be an integral part of Warhol's esthetic too."

"And it was," Len interjected. "Did you see any one of his films with Holly Woodlawn?"

"What I don't understand is how they can not even discuss it?"

"What I think is this is a great drawing of a beautiful man. I'm going to have to get it framed."

"What's a shame is it isn't signed. He usually does sign his stuff, doesn't he?"

"You know, he is breaking the law when he uses those subway spaces. I'll bet someone interrupted him before he could sign it. It's definitely his work though."

"Oh, yeah, fer shur," JB said, using the vacuous Valley girl pronunciation. "Do me a huge favor, Len. Will you leave that here until you take it off to the framers? I would love to appreciate it myself... just for awhile. Pretty please."

"You know how a please looks isn't going to effect my decision in any way..." He paused for effect. "...but all right, I'll leave it with you for a day or so."

"Thank you, good sir."

"Your welcome." Len plopped down in a chair. "Now, since I've been so generous, how about some tea for Sister Mary Largesse? That's the least you can do."

"I found a new herbal tea. Its called Ginger Twist. Want to try it?"

"Sounds like a great name for a stripper. Sure,

brew away."

JB went into the kitchen to make the drink. "The benefit went great tonight," he shouted back to Len. "You and Lee are a great team."

"Not for much longer. I think she's leaving the show soon."

The water heating up, JB stood in the doorway. "You're kidding. What about her contract? It was for two years wasn't it? Like yours."

"Its not public knowledge yet but her son, Christopher, is ill. He's in Lenox Hill, and not expected to come out of there. Rumor has it she's asked for a compassionate release from the show. Equity's considering it."

JB shook his head. "Is it?" he asked.

"Of course. But that's supposed to be a secret too."

JB was back in the kitchen pouring the hot water over the tea bags. "Well I know about it, so it isn't such a big secret is it? Poor Lee. This right on the heels of losing Tommy." ***

These kinds of conversations were taking place with increasing frequency around New York as more and more men became infected with the AIDS virus. The city had become AIDS central, the epicenter of the quickly spreading disease. By then, mid-Nineteen-eighty-seven there were at least thirty-three thousand American victims so far. World-wide the numbers were so high as to be incomprehensible.

These days you only had to give a raised eyebrow in question to find out if it was AIDS that had attacked the person you were discussing. It almost always was. And there was nothing being done about it. Inaction by those that should care was the order of the day. There was a President in office that wouldn't even say the name of the disease, much less do anything to

---

***This part of JB and Len's conversation can be explained by reading *Dance:Ten Murder:Maybe*, Number 5 in the Bent Mystery series.

eliminate it. And people kept on dying. It was maddening. And that was the reason Len had started attending the meetings of ACT-UP.

Shrinks will tell you that there are five phases to the grieving process. Len was firmly in the anger phase. As were many in the gay community. And the goals of ACT-UP gave them a perfect place to expel the emotion. JB, on the other hand, was maybe a scooch closer to the acceptance phase. He had begun working as a volunteer with Gay Men's Health Crisis in their buddy program. You did what you needed to do to get through the losses.

Chapter 3

STARZY HILLARD HAD taken a suite at The Algonquin Hotel over on West Forty-fourth Street. JB got on the subway at noon and rode it to Grand Central Station, then took the shuttle across to Times Square and Forty-second Street. He walked from there to make their lunch appointment on time. It was only a short walk to Forty-fourth Street and the one-hundred and seventy-four room hotel with its white stone facade and black metal Beaux Arts canopy hovering over the entrance.

As a writer the Algonquin was considered a shrine of sorts for JB and his ilk. It was in the hotel's dining room that from the year Nineteen-nineteen and for ten or so years after the renowned Vicious Circle was in full swing. Luncheons with the likes of Robert Benchley, Dorothy Parker, Alexander Woollcott, Edna Ferber, George Kauffman, and various other literary and theatrical lights of the era were an ongoing occurrence. *The New Yorker* magazine was born from discussions held in the dining room. Witty bon mots and word play flew like flocks of pigeons to the George M. Cohan statue over in Times Square.

JB had visited the lobby of the hotel years before and had a drink in the bar. That was way before he'd had his first book published. He was hoping to soak up some of the renowned writers vital spirits perhaps lounging in the place, but he had never gotten around to eating in the famed dining room.

He'd read that the hotel had recently sold to a group of Japanese investors. JB hoped a renovation was going to be first on their agenda. The hotel had last been fixed up in Nineteen-forty-six when the original owner had passed away. The place was looking a tad shabby for a luxury hotel these forty years later. The lobby was decorated in dark woods and faded flower embossed carpets; soft lighting helping hide the slightly worn and stodgy appearance of the old place. A cat lolled in a specially made bed over by the front desk. Probably the animal was a health hazard but it did give the place a homey atmosphere.

JB went to the reception desk in the dining room, inquired of Starzy, found she hadn't arrived, but was shown to a table right away. She had made a reservation for their luncheon which meant JB wouldn't have to take advantage of the free lunch struggling writers were afforded by the hotel.

The room was crowded with afternoon patrons:

the ladies who lunch, businessmen with their double martinis, handsome young male escorts with their older women, mothers and their children — the melting pot. Water was instantly put down and he was left to look over the menu.

His reading was interrupted by a guttural but gentile "Ah-hum" from a lady's voice. JB looked up expecting to see his lunch companion. Instead it was another young woman. She was bland in a nondescript sort of way, wearing heavy horn rimmed glasses, a scarf over her hair, and a tan and brown tweed overcoat. She held out a copy of his latest book.

JB smiled, flattered that someone had recognized him. He took the book, dug a pen from his coat pocket, and signed with a flourish. He held it out to the girl. "There you are."

She softly said, "Thank you," and turned to walk away.

"No, thank you. It's always a pleasure to meet a reader."

"Oh, I haven't read it. But I'm looking forward to it."

And that gave it away. JB straightened in his seat. "Wait a second. I know that voice." He looked the woman up and down and noticed the black five inch high heels poking out from under the dowdy coat. Then he noticed the perfectly manicured fingernails wrapped around his book. "Come back here, young lady."

She turned back with a grin. "But I fooled you, didn't I?"

Starzy had most certainly fooled him. Without her glamour makeup and pale sugar blond hair she didn't look the sex kitten at all. Just another ordinary girl. A secretary perhaps. One of thousands out on the streets of New York City.

She sat across from him. "In your book you called the character wren like. Did it get it? Was I blah enough?" She was looking for some sort of confirmation — a compliment on her ability. Actors? Jezz.

He should be used to it with Len pulling this same

kind of stunt all the time. It must be an actors only sort of disease, this fetish they have for changing one's appearance. Lawrence Oliver was said to have never used his real nose in any part he ever played.

"You did trick me for a moment. That's surprising. But are you willing to look like this on film? It would play hell with your image."

"That's the problem..."

JB knew she was right. The problem was her career was spinning away from her. Fast. Another couple of films that made no money and she was over. She needed to do something to make the people that mattered sit up and take notice. That she thought JB's book could do that was flattering.

"...It's that image that's destroying me," she went on. "It's become a strait-jacket. You want to see? Watch this."

She took off the glasses, slipped out of her coat, and unknotted the scarf over her hair. She shook her head of blond hair and ran her fingers through to put it in place. She opened her purse, pulled out a lipstick, and quickly ran it over her lips. Then she smiled, and somehow flipped a switch located somewhere inside of her. She looked around the dining room. A light had gone on. She was alive. She shimmered. She glowed. She stood out like a search light at a Hollywood preview.

Within moments a waiter was at the table to take their orders, a second later one of the patrons from another table came over asking for an autograph, then another, then a steady stream of people were intruding on them. A crowd was gathering.

Starzy looked over at JB. There was a tinge of panic at the edge of her eyes. "Can we leave?" she asked.

JB stood and made his way over to her. He grabbed her coat as she stood and with him blockading her they headed for the lobby, leaving the dining room and its impolite customers behind.

There was a time in New York when its denizens were more blasé about celebrities. But with television and the familiarity it bred, even New Yorkers now seemed to think they owned these Hollywood people. They could interrupt. They could stick pieces of paper at them whenever and wherever they wanted. JB had even heard of papers being passed under bathroom stall doors. New York had lost some of its anonymity.

In the lobby JB asked, "Where do you want to go?"

Starzy was getting back into her disguise. As she tied the scarf under her chin she said, "Can we go somewhere else? I've been cooped up in my room for what seems like days."

"Well, how about getting something to eat? That's what we met for wasn't it? And I am hungry. Are you?"

"Starved."

"Okay. I know a place where we'll be able to talk and eat in peace. Come on."

After grabbing a cab and directing it crosstown, JB and Starzy got out at East Sixty-fourth & First Avenue. They stopped at the pizza place on the corner for a slice each, and were at JB's apartment door in under twenty minutes.

"Come on in. Hope you don't mind? It's the only place I could think of where you wouldn't cause a riot. What do you want to drink?"

"Anything will be fine. What a great apartment. It's huge. When I lived here I wasn't so lucky. First, I lived with my brother, and then, when I found my own place, I didn't have anything near this big. Believe it or not, I had an eight by twelve foot room. I and myself were a crowd in the place."

"And I'll bet you paid through the teeth for it too."

"Actually it wasn't all that bad. It was still under rent control."

"Lucky you."

That settled it. The girl was really a New Yorker. Only someone who'd experienced New York apartment living could have a coherent conversation about space and rent in the uber-urban environment.

"How long ago did you leave the city?" JB asked.

"When I'd been here five years and had only made

one-hundred and eighty dollars as an actress. And that was to show my elbow as a background extra on *All My Children*. Somehow Hollywood seemed a better bet."

"They do have that wonderful weather…"

There was a knock on the door. JB answered and found Len, looking as if he'd just stepped from the shower. He was all shiny and neat with his wet hair slicked back. He was dressed in a pink alligator shirt with a pair of Sasson jeans tight to his ass. "I came by to pick up my drawing. It's going to the framers." He breezed by JB and started for the kitchen.

"So soon? I was hoping I'd get a whole day with it."

"You've had more than enough time with my little hunk divine." He stopped short on spotting Starzy. "Oh, I'm sorry. I didn't know JB had company."

Starzy held up a hand and wiggled her fingers. "Hi."

"Len, meet Starzy Hillard. This is Len Matthews."

JB found it fascinating watching the two scope each other out. Two actors from different coasts. Both considered stars, but in different areas of the business: movies and theater. Clams and mussels. Whose ego was the bigger? Whose star was the more corpulent between them? Was she an interloper on his turf? Did Len have to go pee in every corner to mark his territory? They didn't actually snarl at each other, but JB was wondering where his spray bottle of water was just in case he needed it.

"I've seen you. Hollywood, right?"

"I've watched you on stage for years. What an honor it is to meet you."

Crisis avoided. She was allowing herself to be subservient to him. He got to be the alpha-star.

"Thanks. I've seen your work too. I'm not so sure the movies have all that much to do with acting, however. Much more to do with cheekbones and keylights…"

JB jumped in. There were times Len didn't know when to stop, and he could be a major theatre snob when confronted with a Hollywood type. Movies verses

Theatre. Hollywood versus New York. Gomorrah with palm trees or Sodom with subways.

"We were just talking about that. Starzy was telling me she started her career here in New York."

"Yes, but work was scarce so I decided to try to make it out in California."

"It seems to have worked out very well for you," Len said.

"Oh, I've got money now, and some notoriety, but they don't take me very seriously out there."

Len raised an eyebrow. "I hate to point this out, but isn't that a bit of a common cliché? Every starlet out there must have the same complaint."

"And every starlet would be right, Mr. Matthews. But I'm not going to let them beat me. That's why I want to option JB's book, get a script, and show them I'm not just some Ann-Margret wanna-be."

"As Ms. Margret did herself with her version of Blanche in *Streetcar* a couple of years ago. She got an Emmy for it."

"I was thinking of her in her *Bye, Bye Birdie* period. There was some director somewhere slobbering all over her on that movie."

"Early in her career. She still had to prove herself."

"And that's what I want to do with this part. That is if JB will sell me the rights to his second book. Will you, JB?"

Len turned to JB. "What rights?" He turned back to Starzy. "Since I'm one of the two protagonists in his books I have some interest..."

"Wait, so you're the Len in the books. I don't know why I didn't see that. Of course."

JB spoke again. "Yes, to my utter and continuing chagrin he is the other character from the series. And he won't let me forget it. To answer your question, Len, we were discussing her optioning my second book for the movies. If she can get a script that is. And since I own the copyright on my books you don't have much say in any deal I might make for them."

"Interesting. You would play the rich daughter then?"

"And she could carry off the plain Jane part of it, Len. She proved that to me earlier."

Len sat on the couch, crossed one leg over the other, and picked at a piece of lint on his knee. "A question. What do you propose to do about the two gay leads in the novel?"

Starzy blithely answered; unaware of the trap he'd set for her. "There will have to be some extensive re-writing of all the characters. It's really only the basic plot I'm interested in."

JB sat next to Len. "I didn't realize that..." Trap sprung

Starzy suddenly looked worried, belatedly realizing she may have stepped on a sensitive toe. She smiled. "Not that I would mind having gay characters in the movie, it's just who would play them? Not many men in Hollywood will even consider playing a gay character."

"That's true, Len. Look at *Less Than Zero*. The movie came out only this week and the book's bisexual lead has somehow become magically straight in the transition. Even *Tootsie* went to extraordinary lengths to make sure you knew Dustin Hoffman was straight. And *Inside Daisy Clover* with Redford, and..."

"And on and on. All the way back to Edward Everett Horton being..." He clicked two fingers in the air. "...*almost* married in *The Gay Divorcee*. Face it, Hollywood doesn't like discussing 'it', They only want to snigger at it."

"There is *Maurice* to consider? I just saw it, and it's a beautiful example of how to approach the subject."

"Well, it's a start I have to admit, but it's English, and so restrained you'd think you were watching Aunt Hagatha's high tea not an unrequited homosexual love affair."

JB turned to Starzy. "So the two main characters in my book would end up with a Butch and Sundance bro-mance whitewash? You'd basically be eviscerating the entire motive behind the book?"

"So you'll sell me the rights?" Starzy was either being completely disingenuous or she seriously didn't see the problem.

JB shook his head. "I'm not so sure. I'll need to think about it. I'll tell you what. We'll need to get our lawyers involved, no matter what, won't we? A lot depends on what's expected from me. So maybe we should set up meetings with them before I make any decision."

The disappointment on Starzy's face was obvious. The woman was not happy. She was used to getting what she wanted — Hollywood could spoil people that way — and here was the very thing she wanted slipping away from her. It just didn't compute in that sun soaked brain of hers.

Len stood. "Well, that's your choice, JB, since I have no say in the matter. I'll just take my drawing and leave." He nodded at Starzy, a slight smile on his lips — as if making a snap without actually snapping.

He went over to the wall and began to pull out the pins, then began to carefully roll the large drawing.

A smile similar to Len's appeared on Starzy's face. She had a bargaining chip. There was a possible trade to be made. A tit for a tat. A "I'll give you something, so you'll give me what I want" exchange. She had finally realized she really needed to get Len on to her side if there was any chance of a deal. So it was him she had to win over. And with what she had she might get her book option after all. She said to him, "You really like that artist don't you? It's a Jathan, right?"

"Yes, it is. He's very talented."

"But to go so far as to rip it right out of the subway. You must really like his work."

"What's your point?"

"How would you like to meet him?"

Both JB and Len said "What?"

"I know him. Very well in fact."

"Not to burst your bubble, my dear, but nobody knows him. He's a mystery man, and he hasn't been seen by anyone. He does all his work at night when there's no one around."

"But I know his work very well. I've seen it most of my life. Jathan is my brother. Well, not really, but like a brother."

Len's interest was piqued. "Really? And you could get us a meeting with him?"

"I just have to call and see if he available." Starzy could already see herself crossing the finish line. Len was going to be her bitch.

JB was also intrigued. At least enough so that he would become complicit with Starzy in this seduction of Len she was pulling.

"Len, maybe you could get him to sign your drawing." JB turned to Starzy. "Do you think he'd do that?"

"I don't see why not." She could feel the laurel wreath being placed on her head. The crowds were cheering.

Len continued to roll the drawing. "You actually know Jathan?" Doubt colored the question.

"I do."

"And you're willing to take us to meet him?" That was it. He was snagged. Hooked. In the net. Stuffed and mounted on the wall.

"I am. Of course, we'll have to discuss how grateful you'll be later, okay?" She smiled at JB and Len.

There's always a price isn't there? Well played Starzy. JB smiled back, then said, "Well, come on, Len, let's go."

Chapter 4

THE EXPLANATION TO her claim was offered while Starzy, JB and Len were taxiing around the city. First they went to the Algonquin to get the phone number of her alleged relative and then called to make sure the person was home. Len had made it clear he wasn't so convinced about the relationship she was positing. Soon enough they were back into a cab to head down to Ninth Avenue in the meatpacking district where this person had a loft space.

Starzy explained that Jathan's real name was Jay Nathan Holt—thus Jathan would make perfect sense as an artist signature for his work—and although he wasn't a blood related brother he had lived with her family for five full years. He had been an occupant in her house from the age of thirteen until he turned eighteen. Her family name was Hillard. Starzy's actual first name was Susan. Her parents had, to help make ends meet in a barely getting by household, taken in troubled kids from Social Services in her hometown of West Orange, NJ. There were sometimes as many as six or seven welfare kids living in her house at any one time.

Starzy had grown up in that overflowing house of ever changing people, and Jay Nathan was just another one of the kids who came and stayed. She was twelve then. A year younger than him when he arrived. They found in each other kindred spirits, and so grew up together in that chaotic atmosphere. With attention spread so thinly in the household Susan and Jay Nathan used each other to support their separate dreams and ambitions.

Jay Nathan, Starzy went on to explain, was a good kid who'd lost his mother to a car accident when he was only six. There was a father who went to drink and excess out of his guilt for causing the accident, and Jay Nathan ended up in the welfare system because there were no other relatives to take him when the father could no longer care for him.

After his initial seven years in the system, he'd been lucky to finally be sent to stay with the Hillards. These people were a good match for a teenage boy just discovering who he was and what his talents were.

Jay Nathan was a quiet kid who had shown artistic leanings from the very beginning. He was always drawing with the colored pencils and crayons he had been supplied or was able to scrounge. His early promise had caused the Hillards to enroll him in art classes at the local art museum where he had flourished under the tutelage provided. He had ended up doing all the graphics for the high school yearbook all three years he was in school, and then began doing freelance paid commercial work for local businessmen his last year in town. When he became of age he moved away and settled in New York City, attending first the Art Students League and then working for a series of ad agencies in their art departments. He had kept in touch with Starzy all the while, even putting her up in his own apartment when she followed him to the city to look for acting work a year later. They had become exactly like the brother and sister she claimed him to be, and they continued to maintain their relationship until that day.

"Wait a minute, young woman, are you sure that the person you're describing is the same person that's doing this subway art? The illegal, outsider, avant-garde, underground, subway art?"

JB scoffed. "What's the matter, Len, doesn't the man she's talking about fit your expectations?"

"Well, no, not exactly. The Jathan I've been thinking about is one of those young hip downtown graffiti art freaks. You've seen them, JB. Wearing black hooded sweatshirts, in low cut jeans almost falling off their asses, a backward baseball cap on their heads, with a spray can of paint in their back pockets. She's describing a Mr. WASPY type. A preppie with a paint brush."

"Every artist has to start somewhere, and pay the bills while he does." Starzy said, defending him.

"She's right, Len. Even Andy Warhol began as a shoe fashion illustrator, and Keith Haring has designed loads of posters for commercial reasons."

Starzy added, "Jay Nathan has had to keep his own life together all by himself, even while he was trying to establish himself in the New York City art world. And its finally starting to happen for him..." She obviously was protective of him, and seemed stung by Len's derogatory opinion of her brother.

Len quickly explained. "No, no. I didn't mean it as a put down of him, my dear. I just meant he doesn't fit any of the familiar pigeonholes. And I guess

I'm stereotyping, aren't I? Pots and kettles calling each other darker colors. And that's wrong. I am sorry."

    The cab pulled up to the front of one of the Greek Revival buildings prevalent in the downtown neighborhood. The street level was given over to an actual meat processing company, one of the few remaining in the once busy area. Right then the only sound was the flapping in the breeze of the heavy plastic strips that covered the open doors like beaded curtains as men went in and out. A single man with a garden hose spritzed the cobblestone street, washing away that morning's blood and offal. It was quiet right then. At four AM, however, there had to be an unholy racket for the residents who lived above this slaughterhouse. There would have been burly crowds of men shouting to be heard over the din of trucks loading and unloading carcasses of cow and pig.

    The neighborhood itself was in transition —as New York City itself would always be — moving from a longstanding industrial environment to a newer residential one. Lofts were being carved from extinct manufacturing business's on the upper floors and small boutique's were taking over the bottom stalls, pushing the older butcher and processing plants to relocate elsewhere.

    Nighttime in the surrounding area could be downright dangerous. Transvestites and working girls shared the streets with drug dealers and club kids. The Mineshaft had been a popular gay club in the area but had been closed several years before when the burgeoning health crisis had panicked city officials. A disco had taken over an old warehouse around the corner, and the Hellfire, a multi-gender sex club, was located only a few blocks over.

    Starzy, JB, and Len went to a door at the side of the building and buzzed for entrance. The latch was released, and they stepped inside. A white sheetrocked stairwell with red painted metal stairs took them up to the third floor where there wasn't plain white sheetrock anymore. The floor's occupant had painted a mural on the landing. It was a homage to Paul Cadmus and his gay encoded painting *The Fleets In* from the Nineteen-thirties. Much more explicit than his this picture was of very hot carousing sailors on leave in ass hugging white bell-bottoms hitting on and picking up sex charged male hustlers in a garish urban park setting. They were a riot of colors leading to a large black tin plated double door hanging on a track.

"Well, I guess I was wrong, this certainly is Jathan's work. I'd know these sexy men of his anywhere."

"I told you." Starzy used her fist and banged on the door.

A minute later it was slid back and they got their first glimpse of the mysterious Jathan.

He was in his mid-twenties, tall and well built, with a broad square chest. Tight taut toned muscles under a plain white T-shirt. Strong arms and blocky shoulders, narrow hips amd substantial thighs, either from running or being a gym habitué. He had blond hair, a yellower shade than Warhol's platinum. It swept back in waves from an uncreased wide forehead. There was an aquiline nose, a strong chin, and piercing eyes. Good looking, if not a GQ model beauty, he could look either mean or sweet, depending on how the light struck the planes of his face. He took Starzy in his arms for a hug and then held out his hand as she introduced both Len and JB. His voice was soft but strong with a confidence that animated his speech. "Hello, a pleasure to meet you. Suzy, I'm so glad to see you. Come in, come in." He stood aside and gestured for them to enter the loft.

It was a huge space, with a floor to ceiling muslin curtain blocking off the back part. Presumably his studio was behind the curtain, which was hung with standard shower rings from a taut wire strung wall to wall. It had previously been used as a floor covering and was a Jackson Pollock like span of colorful paint drips and spills. The front of the open loft was set up with a kitchen over to the side, a living area, and a bed behind that. The furniture was piecemeal, good pieces picked up from thrift shops and auctions it looked like. An overstuffed Forties couch and chair, a modern coffee table. The bedroom was a mattress and box spring on the floor with Indian sari fabrics draped around it like a harem out of the Arabian Nights. A tall Victorian veneered armoire stood at the side of the bed.

JB was pretty sure Jathan couldn't pass for a straight guy, not with his place decorated the way it was. Far too nicely laid out, even if there wasn't much worth more than thirty-five bucks in the entire place. Only another queer would decorate like this, or could do so much with so little. It sure wasn't a man cave. Done with far too much taste for any single straight guy. They'd usually settle for their parents old sectional couch and an Army trunk to hold the TV, with a beer can pyramid in the corner.

"Great space you have here," Len said. Jathan, from the kitchen area, answered, "Thanks. I found it a couple of years ago, for real cheap. No one wanted to live down here then. It's still kinda iffy around here, but on the way up. And I can still afford it. I can't tell you what an honor it is to have you here, Mr. Matthews." He came to the living area with a tray holding a pitcher of lemonade and four glasses. "Will this do?"

"More than we expected. Please call me Len. That is if I can call you Jathan?"

Len was gushing like a schoolgirl. Jathan was grinning from ear to ear. JB was surprised but amused. It was a fan meeting another fan. Mutual aficionado. This wasn't normal for Len. He was far more used to receiving favor not giving it. If those two continued in this vein it could get very sticky around here real fast.

Starzy said, "You said on the phone that you had some good news. What was it, sweetheart?" She was oblivious to the two men and their liking for each other. If adoration wasn't aimed at her she wasn't interested. JB then realized he was standing in the middle of a gaggle of narcissists. Or was it a swarm? A covey? This group consisted of both up and comers and more established conceits. Actors, starlets, artists...and if forced to admit it, even a writer. As for Jeremy Bent's narcissism Jeremy Bent would discuss that in his forthcoming book titled *Jeremy Bent*. He fit right in.

"Huh? Oh, I got an art job, Suzy. A really good one. For a shitload of money."

Money was obviously a concern for him. The starving artist thing, of course.

"I'm going to do the big display window at *A Different Read*, that gay bookstore over on Hudson Street. The manager there called out of the blue and hired me. At an enormous commission. Enough so I won't have to take any more freelance advertising jobs this year. Money won't be a problem for once. Isn't that great?"

"Terrific. I'm happy for you, honey."

"What about your anonymity?" Len asked. "I thought that people weren't supposed to know who you were. Won't a job like that blow your cover?"

"I can work on it at night if I want to. And when I do have to work where I can be seen I have this..." He went to a shelf on the far wall, and picked up a leather hood to show them. A Spanish wrestler's mask it was black with red pieces sewn around the eyes and surrounding the mouth, and yellow lightning bolts stitched on both sides. "I got it last year at this Santaria shop on the Upper West Side. Cool, huh?"

"Very..."

"Anyway, I'm not so concerned about the hiding thing anymore. I did it mostly to protect my advertising clients. They wouldn't hire an illegal graffiti artist, and I need the money they pay when I do work for them. So I did the subway drawings on the sly. Now that I'm getting paid to do my own work, maybe I won't have to hide so much."

"Speaking of your drawings, I do have a ulterior motive for meeting you. Beyond the pleasure of that, I mean." My God, JB was thinking, roll up your pant's legs, it's getting deep in here. "I have one of your drawings..." And Len explained about the unsigned piece. "So, would you sign it for me?"

"Sure. Of course. I'd be thrilled." JB gagged a

little. "Come on. You can spread it out here."

He went over to the curtain and walked it across the room. Behind it was, as JB had suspected, his studio. There were four windows along the back wall which provided enough light for the artist to work with. In front was a large table made of plywood and two by fours nailed together like a Louise Bourgeois art installation. Along the side was a series of storage racks to hold finished pieces. Behind the work table stood an easel covered with a tarp. Jathan moved a few items on the table and Len unrolled his poster. Bean bags weighted with shot quickly held the corners down.

"I remember this. The cops were coming, so I had to leave it. But it is actually already signed. Look in the fish tail. I hide my signature on every piece I do. It's sort of like Al Hirschfeld and his NINA's. See?" He pointed to a set of swirls in the merman's tail and sure enough they spelled out his initials.

"Aren't you the sneaky one? I would have never seen that." They laughed together. JB shook his head. This was getting nauseating.

"You do have a lot of finished work." JB pointed to the bins that rose to the ceiling along the side wall. They were stuffed to the gills with stretched finished canvases, representing what had to be many many hours of work. There had to be at least two hundred paintings on those racks.

"As Gloria Swanson once said, 'I'm ready for my close up, Mr. DeMille.' I know I'll get a one man show someday, and I'm ready for it. These are the better ones. There are others that I've destroyed. They didn't come up to standard. My standard at least."

Jathan picked up a piece of chalk and leaned over Len's drawing. He signed it with a flourish on the left hand corner. Then put the date under his signature. "There. Is that okay? Or do you want it personalized?"

Len reached out and covered Jathan's hand. "No, that will be fine. Thank you so much." JB felt the bile churn a little in his stomach. A taste of it hit the back of his throat. "How can I repay you? Perhaps dinner?

Tonight?"

"Uh, I'd like to, but maybe another time. I should be with Suzy tonight. I don't see her often enough."

Len turned to her. "You must come too. In fact, all of us should go. I insist. We'll make a party of it. To celebrate your new commission. How about it?"

They decided to eat at *The Sazerac House*, a bar and grill located in one of the landmark eighteen-twenty houses over in the Village.

Chapter 5

IT WAS NINE in the morning a week later that JB heard a knock on his door and found Len standing there when he opened it. Behind him stood Jathan Holt, the artist. Interesting. JB hadn't realized that the two of them had become such fast friends, although he should have guessed after witnessing their first meeting. This looked to be a budding affairette between them? It was never much more than that for Len. He tended to go through men the way cold sufferers went through tissues. Men were many and disposable for him. One of the advantages of being well-known.

"We're on our way to the unveiling of Jathan's artwork at the bookstore. Want to come along?"

"Uh, I'm not dressed..." JB was in standing in the doorway in pajama bottoms and a T-shirt.

"We can wait. They're not showing his painting until eleven. There's plenty of time. If you'll give us breakfast."

Jathan, from behind Len, said, "A bowl of cereal will do. He had a single egg of questionable age and a jar of cocktail olives in his refrigerator."

"With which any competent chef could have made an omelet out of. I'm simply not the Julia Child type." Len shrugged.

"I held the egg to my ear. I heard pecking from the inside."

"Chicken Fricassee then"

"I have cereal, and milk. Come on in. I'll go get dressed."

JB got them the ingredients for their breakfast and went to the bathroom, where he managed a quick whore's bath and a quicker shave. A pair of button fly jeans, and a denim jacket over the T-shirt had him dressed. Loafers without socks gave a casual edge to the look. He packed his leather backpack and was ready to go in under twenty minutes.

They took the subway down to Christopher Street and walked through the Village over to Houston Street where the bookstore was located. A small crowd, made up mostly of the store employees, had gathered out front to watch the unveiling. A young man in chinos and a knitted plaid sweater vest was pacing back and forth, checking his watch every few minutes. Jathan went over to him. They had a hurried conversation, and then he turned and came back to stand with Len and JB.

"That's the assistant manager," he explained. "He's

worried because the manager isn't here yet..." Jathan went on to say that the store manager was the one who was behind the window decoration and the one who had hired him. His idea was to use Jathan's artwork as the backdrop for a newly published book on the New York Outsider Graffiti Art scene. The manager, John Weatherwax by name, and Jathan had last talked the night before as he had finished up his painting. Weatherwax had said then that he would introduce Jathan when he opened the window this morning. Now here it was close to opening and he wasn't anywhere to be found. The assistant was worried. He felt it wasn't like John to miss out on something like this. And he wasn't answering his home phone, so there was no telling where he might be.

It got to be a quarter hour after the appointed time to open and Weatherwax still hadn't shown up. Jathan left his place with JB and Len again, took the assistant by the arm and led him inside the store. There he suggested that the assistant should step up and do the ceremony himself. Being inside also gave Jathan a chance to get ready for his own introduction by getting into the Santeria mask he was wearing to disguise his identity.

The assistant manager took it upon himself and made an executive decision. Since they were losing business by waiting, and Jathan's was the most logical idea he'd heard so far, he decided to go ahead with the unveiling. He went outside to stand in front of the fifty or sixty people that had gathered, took hold of the microphone that had been set up there, and welcomed them.

"...and it is with great pleasure I introduce to you the artist himself...the amazing Jathan."

The crowd applauded and Jathan came out from the store in his mask and spoke for a quick moment. The assistant used the time to go back inside the store and get prepared for the unveiling by standing at the control panel. When Jathan was done speaking he asked him to push the button that would raise the motorized curtain that covered the inside of the window.

It started to rise. There was a mummer of expectation from the crowd.

Which soon turned to horror as the curtain continued to go up and revealed the bloodied beaten body of a man propped against the back wall in a twisted parody of the Jathan painted figure behind him. Both of his arms were extended wide, one leg was bent over the other as if the dead man was doing some type of macabre dance across the window. A shuffle off of the mortal coil instead of to Buffalo. His head was turned to the side, his mouth stretched by rigor to a grim and toothy grin, seemingly laughing at his own visit from Mr. Death.

JB rushed through the crowd up to the window, used his open hands to beat on the glass to get the assistant's attention inside, and shouted, "Push the reverse button. Make the curtain go back down."

The stunned young man did as he was instructed and the curtain began to slowly slide back down, finally covering the grisly scene from the onlookers who hadn't turned and fled as the scene had unfolded.

A few moments later JB, Len, and Jathan were inside the store and headed for the entrance to the window. Standing in the doorway was the assistant looking as if he was about to go into a faint. Len reached him first and took him under the arms to help keep him standing upright.

JB asked him, "Who was it? Do you know who the dead man is?"

He nodded. "It's John. Mr. Weatherwax I mean. The manager. There's a stain on his chest. Red. He's been stabbed. Or shot. Something." His hand went to his mouth. "Oh, my God. I've got to call the police."

Len shifted so the young man was now hanging off his shoulder. "I'll take you to the office. You can sit there, and make your call." He looked at JB. "Okay?"

"A good idea. I'm going to take a look in there before anything gets disturbed." JB pointed to the window. "Maybe the killer made a mistake and left behind a clue. That's all a clue is, really. A mistake made by the perpetrator. We only have to figure out how to read what's there."

Len went off with the assistant in tow while JB and Jathan stepped up into the window. Inside it was quiet and somber. With the curtain down and the lights off it was also dark and difficult to see anything. "Can you get us some light? I need to see what I'm looking at."

A second later the overhead floodlights went on and the window exploded with sharp color. The garish brights of Jathan's painting colors had an almost neon effect up close, strobing in the bright lights. The body was profiled as if a grotesque version of Jathan's cartoon like painting. The dead man's blood stained chest almost pulsated in the glare. A stream of red sluiced down his chest onto his tan pants, pooling at his stocking clad feet.

"The assistant was right. He was stabbed and then bled out. That could have taken hours to happen. When did you last talk to him, Jathan?"

JB was again confounded by how easily and seamlessly he'd slipped into this detection mode of his. Why was it so damn easy for him to appraise these situations and then figure out the puzzle that was offered? It was some sort of innate instinct that took over when he was confronted by crime. Perhaps in one of his past lives he was a Pinkerton detective — or simply a raving busybody and smart-ass sticking his nose in where it was unwanted.

Jathan responded to his question. "Last night, right as I was leaving for the night. He was going to stay to set up the book display..."

"Which hasn't been done. The books are still stacked over by the entrance. So his killer arrived before he could get to do that. What time was it that you left?"

"Around ten. I went right from here to Len's. We had a late dinner."

And a raunchier sort of tete-a-tete after eating, JB guessed. Which explained Jathan being with Len that morning at his door.

"But Weatherwax would have locked the store up after you left, wouldn't he? If he didn't that must be how his assailant got in. Otherwise why would he have let anyone in?"

"No, he couldn't have locked up then. The store closes at eleven. So it wouldn't have been locked yet."

"Then that's how his killer got in. And got out by mixing in with the other customers. And nobody would have thought to check the windows before closing."

JB started looking closer at the window space. There was a white sheet of heavy paper on the floor, which explained why Weatherwax was not wearing shoes. He wouldn't have wanted to leave shoe prints on the pristine clean display area. However, it looked to JB like the killer had no such qualms. There was a clear set of shoe prints coming in and walking around the space. The pattern the shoes left behind made JB think they were probably from a pair of Dr. Dexter boots; the rubber soles of the brand had a distinctive pattern that was easily recognized. That would have been the killer's first mistake, and JB's first clue. It also meant the killer was most likely young and fairly hip, considering how trendy the Dexter brand boots were. Comparing the shoe print size to his own feet told JB the killer was about a size ten. Clue number two. JB was just slightly over six foot tall, so the killer was also in that range. What other clues had the culprit left behind?

JB noticed over at the far side of the display space, high up in a corner, a video camera. It was store security to the rescue. The angle the camera was set at would have given a full view of the window and the immediate area outside.

"Jathan, while you were working in here last night was the curtain down or up?"

"Up. Why?"

"I was just wondering. Then you must have been wearing your mask, right? Since the public could have watched you as you worked."

He nodded. JB then guessed that the camera was

most likely working also. A manager would have it on if people were still in the store. This was giant clue number three. It meant there was a videotape of the event itself. But how was he going to get to see the tape?

While JB was wondering about that the first of the police the assistant called arrived. Now that really was going to make it difficult. Stick a cop in the center of things and no real investigating by any outsider would be accomplished. JB heaved a sigh as the cop brusquely took over and hustled both him and Jathan out of the window. Another cop, stationed at the entrance of the store, directed them to the office where the assistant manager and Len were waiting.

They took the center stairs down and headed to the back of the basement sales area where the office was located. They passed table after table of remaindered books stacked four deep and twenty high. A bibliophilic graveyard of unfulfilled promise, every price slashed book representing some struggling author's dreams smashed upon cut rate shoals.

Once they got to the office door another uniformed cop opened it for them and ushered them in. Len was sitting talking to a plainclothes officer who was making notes on their conversation. Another officer was talking with the assistant manager. Neither cop was anyone JB recognized from any of his other dealings with the police, nor was either of them anything to write home about. Just workaday police detectives, doing their routine duties and waiting for their pensions to kick in. But they did seem to know their jobs and were going about this initial questioning in a completely professional manner.

JB took a seat in one of the rolling office chairs to wait his turn. He looked around the office. It was tiny and cramped, simply cut with a plywood partition from the back few feet of the store. Pressed wood shelves on metal brackets ran along the upper section of the wall. They were filled with cardboard boxes of supplies; reams of paper, printed invoices, plastic covered binders. A plain white laminate covered slab ran along the wall lower down and served as a communal desk. The other wall was decorated with advertising one sheets for various publishers latest books and a large cork board with employee notices attached.

At the rear was a separate desk with a bank of TV screens hanging above it. The store's surveillance center. Twelve screens, three rows of four, were aimed at various locations around the premises. One of them was showing the display window; which, at that moment, was picturing the dead man leaning against the wall. Two other cops had arrived since JB and Jathan had left. One was wearing a lab coat and was probably from the coroner's office.

Underneath each TV screen was a VCR recording machine, so there were twelve separate cassettes for each working day. Then there had to be another couple of sets of tapes also, since a VCR machine could only record six hours at a time at its slowest speed. That was a lot of cassettes to keep around, so they must rotate their supply. Over at the side was a tall two door tan metal cabinet where JB guessed they were stored. Now how was he going to gain access to them?

It looked certain he wasn't. Not anytime soon anyway. The cops finished with Len and the assistant and then turned to JB and Jathan. They only asked a few basic questions: name, address, reason for being on the scene, and wrote down their answers. After that the officers told them they could leave. Then asked that they come to the station the next morning to make a more complete statement. JB, Len and Jathan were standing outside the store within the hour.

"Well, what do you want to do now?"

"Anyone up for food?"

JB checked his watch. It was lunchtime. "How about One Potato? Its close."

Chapter 6

AS JB'S HAMBURGER was put before him he spoke more to himself than the other two men at the table, "Damn."

Len looked over. "Your hamburger isn't cooked right? The owner is right over there. I'll get her for you."

Said owner was nursing a Bloody Mary and leaning against the wraparound bar talking with a group of her cronies. A short bulky blond woman she was one very boisterous lesbian with a laugh that reminded JB of Phyllis Diller. She was a flannel dyke holding court. Rumored to be the sister of a famous movie star she was supposed to have been set up in the cafe by her wealthy sibling. That kind of thing happened often in the Village; relatives of famous people turning up with their own business's in the gay ghetto. The brother of Kaye Ballard ran a well-known art gallery on Christopher Street. Giving relatives a business to work in seemed a good way to keep them out of the limelight and still have them taken care of. Just another form of the proverbial closet. The brother of a famous dancer had a chic little clothing store across the street from the gallery.

"No, that isn't it, Len. The burgers fine." He picked up a steak fry and took a bite. "I'm futzing because I can't figure out a way to get hold of last night's security tape from the bookstore. With the cops crawling all over the place they'll be sure to confiscate it."

"Why do you want it?" Jathan asked between bites of his chicken salad sandwich. "Does it have some special significance?"

"It certainly does. It probably shows the actual murder. And the person who did it. You told us that the manager was still there when you left last night, right? Well, that window he was in had a camera on it. I spotted it earlier. It surely would have filmed last nights events. Unless the cameras were turned off."

Len swallowed a bite of his onion ring. "They weren't. The assistant manager changed the tapes when we went down to the office this morning. At my suggestion, I might add."

"What are you saying?"

"That I told him it was a good idea to stick to his regular routines of the store. It would help take his mind off the manager being dead. The guy was a wreak, but he went ahead and changed the tapes. All twelve of them. One at a time. Including that display window video you're so interested in. Watching him do it was about as exciting as listening to a queen do a Bette Davis impression." He raised a hand and twirled it. "What a drag...," he camped, using Ms. Davis's signature speech cadence. Len then leaned over and picked up his backpack. He started rummaging in it. Back to his own voice he said, "It was easy enough to switch this with another cassette." He set a VCR tape on the table. "You know, if this acting thing hadn't worked out I would've made a hell of a pickpocket."

"You mean to say that's the tape from the store?"

"I'm saying if my pockets were lined with rubber I could steal soup."

"But how did you know..."

"Even now I could be the Robin Hood of wit. I could steal from the clever and give to the dull."

"Will you get a grip, Len. How the hell did..."

"Did I know you would be interested in that tape? After all these years of hanging around you I have a good idea of how your mind works, JB. You get to play Miss Marple again, don't you, sweetie? That must make you very happy. You've got yourself invited to the murder, again, right?"

"Actually, no. I'm the uninvited guest at this shindig."

"Well, its not the first time is it? Anyway, when we got down to the office I saw the rack of TV's. Then I noticed the one TV showing the window. It was still live and showing you and Jathan looking around..." He turned to Jathan. "You look very good on TV by the way. You should consider giving up the whole disguise thing."

JB ordered, "Get back to your story."

"What's left to tell? I know a clue when I see one, JB. So I snagged that silly cassette for you. I knew from the git-go you were going to look into this murder. You couldn't pass it up. It's just not in your nature."

"Said the scorpion to the frog," JB said, referring to the old fable. "But there's a problem."

"What?"

He held up the tape. "It's called tampering with the evidence, Len. In this case, actually stealing it."

"Well, it isn't like we haven't done that before

either..."

"You can go to jail for it, Len."

"You mean the cops would arrest us?"

"Faster than Velveeta on trailer trash. And what you mean *us*, kemo-sabe?" JB said, using the punchline to a different old joke. He sat back and popped a fry in his mouth, rather enjoying Len's discomfort for the moment.

"What can I do, JB?"

"What *we*..." JB said, emphasizing the we to let Len know he had escaped the hook, "...have to do is to get this tape back to the cops."

"How are *we*..." Len said, using the same emphasis as JB. "...going to accomplish that?"

"I still have to make a formal statement to that homicide detective we talked to. We can leave the tape in his office tomorrow. As understaffed and discombobulated as the police can be, he'll just think it got there by accident. Things are misplaced all the time I'll bet." He picked up the tape. "Of course, we'll leave it after I get a dupe made off this original."

✻✻✻

The three of them finished their lunch then cabbed it back to their respective homes. Jathan back to his loft. JB and Len on to there own neighborhood on the Upper East Side. Len went directly to his apartment while JB walked over to the Avenue and went into the local video store. He wanted to have the duplicate tape made right away. He would pick it up later that day.

JB was back home in less than an hour. He made himself a cup of tea, and had just sat down at his computer to work some when the phone rang. If he had been in the middle of a plot, or a paragraph, or even a line in his latest manuscript, he would have let the answering machine get the call, but he hadn't even started so he picked up. It was Starzy Hillard on the other end of the line.

He'd expected her to call and ask him to a meeting with her lawyers. They still needed to talk about that option she wanted on his book; which he had to admit he hadn't made a decision about yet. Instead what he got when he answered was a soggy and tearful Starzy asking for his help.

There had been a calamity. Jathan had been arrested and taken to the police precinct where he was being held until he could be taken to court for arraignment. Starzy wanted JB to help her get him out of jail without all the attendant publicity her being there would engender.

"Arrested. He got caught in the subways, doing one of his drawings, didn't he? That's only a misdemeanor, Starzy. It's not a big deal. I mean can they even hold him on something so minor?"

"No, JB. It's so much worse. He's being charged with murder. That job he had. Doing the window. When it was unveiled this morning, the manager of the bookstore was found in there. Dead."

"I knew that. I was there when it happened."

"Oh, I didn't know. JB, the police have arrested Jay Nathan for it. They think he killed that man. But he couldn't have..."

Chapter 7

"GODDAMN IT JB, Jathan couldn't have done it. He was with me. Don't you see? I'm his alibi. How could he have killed anyone when he was upstairs, in my bed, wrapped snugly in my arms?"

"Sounds very cozy."

Len, in the midst of a meltdown, was pacing around JB's living room.

"It's absolutely ridiculous, that's what it is. Good God, the cops in this city are so damn incompetent. I just don't see how could they even think that he did it?"

JB, sitting on the couch watching him wander back and forth, answered with the truth as he had just heard it, "Because they have evidence, Len. It seems there was another camera in the store that caught Jathan going into the window..."

"It wasn't him."

"...and then coming out of the window with a knife in his hand. That tended to give them a more than evident conclusion to jump to."

※※※

JB had gone straight over to Starzy's hotel right after her call. On his advice she had called her lawyer who, as JB arrived, was on the phone with the police getting the pertinent information about Jathan that JB was now passing on to Len.

The lawyer had advised them that Jathan was indeed in very serious trouble. Like most lawyers he could state the obvious as if it was all his personal revelation and not standard operating procedure. He then informed them Jathan was being held on first degree murder and he wasn't going to be let go, not until there had been a bail hearing anyway. So, the lawyer's advice was the usual "there is nothing we can do right now." They would simply have to wait. For that he charged three hundred dollars an hour. He did add one original piece of advice. That Starzy should look into getting a first rate defense lawyer for Jathan.

※※※

Len was still agitated. "Well, we have to go to the police and tell them what I know, JB. I'll go to the station with you tomorrow. That'll put a stop to this."

JB wasn't thrilled throwing cold water at Len's righteous anger, but someone had to be practical about this. "Len, are you absolutely sure that Jathan was with you all night? Could he have got up from bed and left the apartment at some point? While you were asleep, maybe? You do sleep like the dead, you know. Elephants having a spring cotillion next to the bed wouldn't wake you."

"No...," then he hesitated. "Well, maybe...Oh shit, I don't know." He stopped pacing and plopped onto the couch. "I guess I'm not such a great alibi after all."

"The police are going to want to know about his being with you anyway. So, we'll both still need to go to the station." JB checked his watch. "Hey, the duplicate tape should be ready by now. We can watch it and have a better idea of what really happened at the bookstore last night." JB stood and went over to the door. He took his jacket from the coat rack. "You coming?"

"I'll wait. Didn't you say Starzy was coming over? There should be someone here if she does."

"Right. I won't be long."

※ ※ ※

JB picked up the tape and was back at his apartment in under thirty minutes. But in that time Starzy had indeed arrived. Len had caught her up on what was going on. She was as eager to see the video as Len and JB were.

"There is no way I will believe that Jay Nathan did this horrible thing," she was saying. "He's not the kind of person who would kill. It's not in him."

"That's what I said, but the police..." Len tsked. "...they seem to think otherwise."

JB held up the tape in his hand. "So, let's see why they're thinking that he did it. Uh, Starzy, if this is what we think it is, it isn't going to be pretty. Are you up to it?"

She nodded and gestured for him to go ahead. JB slipped the cassette into the VCR machine and then went to sit on the sofa next to the other two. They watched intently as the first images came on the screen. Images of JB and Jathan standing in the window talking.

"That's from this morning. I don't get..."

"The tape must have run out from the night before, rewound, and then started taping again covering the earlier scene."

"I hope we didn't lose anything important."

JB took up the VCR remote and hit the fast play button. He watched as his image started moving like a comic stick figure around the window. Then there was a bit of static and the scene changed to the same window the night before, but now it was empty and only catching the occasional window shopper looking in from outside. Another press of the remote and the tape rolled forward again. Finally Jathan, wearing his leather mask, stepped into the frame. After setting out his supplies, he picked up a brush and started to paint on the white expanse of the window's backdrop. He worked diligently and quickly, even more so due to the fast forward feature of the VCR machine.

When Weatherwax stepped into the frame JB pressed a button and the tape slowed to normal speed. They watched as the two men stood talking, seemingly friendly with each other—although what they were saying couldn't be guessed since the video was silent—but there didn't seem to be any reason to suspect what was coming. Then Jathan bent, packed his supplies away, turned, and left the display area. John Weatherwax was alone in the window.

"That's exactly what Jathan said happened. He left and the guy was setting up the books. He was telling the truth." Len slid forward on the couch, leaning in and watching the video intently.

Weatherwax first stood and looked at the backdrop, seemed to approve of it, and then stepped out of frame, presumably to get the boxes of books needed to set up the rest of the display. JB again fast forwarded the tape. When Weatherwax was again in the frame he slowed the tape back to normal. Now JB also slid forward on the couch, joining Len and Starzy as they closely scrutinized what they were watching.

Weatherwax was putting out a set of clear plastic risers when he started and looked up, seeming to be taken by surprise at some noise over to his side. He stopped what he was doing, stood, and turned toward the window entrance. He didn't appear to be fearful or anxious, merely curious. He smiled in welcome when a man wearing a Mexican wrestlers leather mask walked into the frame. Was it him? Was it Jathan? The figure they were seeing was the right height and build, but so were many men. Jathan's stature was what was called average. The mask did a good job of hiding the culprit's face.

As the two men talked the leather masked figure reached up and fiddled at the back of his head. Then he slipped off his mask. JB stopped the tape. It jiggled a little but then held steady. The picture was still, showing the man's face clearly. The man talking with Weatherwax sure as hell looked like Jathan. That or it was a damn good impersonator. But JB wasn't so sure an impersonator could look so very much like Jathan. Impersonators always bore some resemblance to the person they looked like but you could usually tell they weren't the real things. JB and Len had both seen enough Cher drag queens to know the truth of that.

Len slouched back on the couch. "Oh, shit. That's him."

Starzy shook her head. "It doesn't make sense."

"So he was there. Let's see what happens next."

JB set the tape to run forward again. The picture soon showed the two men appear to get into an argument. At least they were gesturing angrily at each other. Weatherwax tried to step past Jathan, presumably to leave the window space, but was stopped when Jathan put his hand on Weatherwax's shoulder. Jathan then pushed him and Weatherwax stumbled backward a step or two. He shook it off and stepped toward Jathan again. But Jathan now had something in his hand. He held it out and with a flick of his wrist a blade appeared. Jathan had drawn a switchblade knife from his pants pocket. He thrust the blade toward Weatherwax. Weatherwax jumped back and put up his hands in surrender, but Jathan didn't stop. Instead, he leaped forward, grabbed Weatherwax by the shoulder, and plunged the knife blade into his stomach.

Starzy yelped, closed her eyes and put her hands over her mouth. JB and Len looked at each other, doubt and incredulity clearly on their faces. They said nothing then, but turned back to the screen. It never ceased to amaze JB how quick and mundane it could all be. Murder was supposed to be some type of horrendous event, a major catastrophe. Shocking in its evil action. But it wasn't. It was quick, and dull, and every day. One moment alive. The next...

Weatherwax's head snapped back, his jaw dropped in a silent scream. His arms grabbed at Jathan, but slid on the slick leather sleeves of his coat. He pushed himself away from Jathan, stepped back, and bent forward, grabbing at his stomach, a wave of pain likely passing through him. Then he spun around to face the camera, reaching a hand out, as if grasping for someone to help. Someone to hold on to him while he died. His turn brought the blood soaked front of his shirt into sharp focus, the white hand clutching at his wound standing out in stark contrast against the widening dark red blood stain. He started to sink toward the floor. But Jathan, instead of letting him fall, stepped forward, took hold of Weatherwax under the arms and walked him backwards toward the back of the window. He laid the slumping now dying man against the back wall then took hold of his face with one hand. Jathan twice slapped him with his other hand in some vain hope to revive him. Jathan then leaned in to check for a heartbeat. He found none. He looked up, as if asking for heavens help. When none appeared he looked over at the door. Toward the exit. He stood, yanked the knife from the unmoving dead body of John Weatherwax, and walked out of the frame.

JB stopped the tape.

"Well, I get why he was arrested."

Starzy shook her head. "I still won't believe it. Regardless of what that shows. Jay Nathan could not have done this."

"Well, does he have a twin then? Because that was certainly one hell of a lookalike. What do you think,

JB?"

JB was still staring at the screen. The picture of the dead man lying against the wall was a flickering image. "I just might agree with you, Starzy." Len threw up his hands in disbelief. "I'll have to study the tape some more, but there's a couple of anomalies in it that need to be looked at..."

Len sat forward. "What the hell, JB? The tape shows clearly that Jathan killed that Weatherwax person. Good God, I slept with a murderer. Does that make me an accessory?"

"Only if he picked you up in the scarf department at Bergdorf's. But there were a couple of things that weren't right. For one, I don't understand why his shoes were different? Did he leave, change shoes, and come back? Why would he do that?"

"What are you talking about? Shoes? What does his footwear have to do with anything?"

JB was hitting the remote, winding the tape back to the part where Jathan first left the window. When he got to it he stopped the tape. "Look there, Jathan is wearing a pair of high top sneakers. Canvas sneakers, not the Dr. Dex's that left those tracks when he came back. Why would Jathan have changed his shoes?"

"Like a lot of New Yorkers maybe he's a slave to fashion? He wanted to match his outfit. He could be a Metrosexual."

JB had to admit Len could be right. There was a new phenomenon around town. A new breed of male walking around New York City. There were gay men. There were straight men. And now there had evolved the gayraight man. A hermaphroditic blending of both gay and straight attributes in one body or mass. He'd arrived after years of being exposed to the high fashion, musical theater, supreme art, exquisite cuisine, and plain old everyday chic to be found leaking freely from the gay culture onto the breeders side all over New York. He was being called a Metrosexual, although JB always thought that the term sounded more like someone who picked up tricks at the Metropolitan Museum of Art.

"But Len, he said he came straight to your place after he left the bookstore. Did he bring a change of clothes with him? Because he's not dressed the same when he kills Weatherwax. Look."

JB had again fast forwarded the tape to the killing. He stopped the tape. "What's he wearing? You're the fashion maven here."

Len looked closer. The killer was wearing a pair of baggy blue jeans, probably a *Bugle Boy* brand, with a heavy chain looped from the front pocket to the back. He had on a white printed T-shirt, with some designer logo emblazoned across its front, and a with a black leather jacket over that. And the now obvious Dr. Dexter shoes. Also the leather mask. "Okay, I'll give you this one. Those are not the same clothes he had on when he came to my place."

Starzy pointed at the screen. "Another thing. The mask isn't the same. The shapes are different on that one he's wearing. Jay Nathan's had lightening bolts on it. Yellow lightening bolts. Remember when he showed it to us. That mask has stars. It isn't the same person. I told you. Jay Nathan didn't do this. I knew it."

"It certainly will cast a great deal of doubt on the police having their killer. But you have to admit the man on the screen does look like Jathan. Is it possible he has a twin, Starzy?"

"I have no idea. He's never mentioned one. But Jay Nathan didn't come to live with my family until he was a teenager. Almost grown. He'd been in the foster care system a lot longer. God knows what happened to him before he came to us. What he might have repressed along the way."

"Then we've got to get this tape to the police. And make sure they watch it. That should get Jathan off the hook for this murder. Len, tomorrow morning, first thing, you and I are going to the station to make our statements. We'll have to figure out some way to get them to watch this tape when we get there."

Chapter 8

"FIRST THING" TO Len was a completely different concept than for JB. Len felt it was sometime between ten AM and three PM, while JB was knocking on Len's door at 9AM. He didn't get an answer. When he laid his ear on the door he could hear Len inside. Snoring. Despite many claims from him to the contrary Len was a first class snoreombulist. If using musical terms JB would hear a thundering arpeggio that would build to a crescendo, and then fade away into a breathy whistle. It was more cacophonous than melodically symphonic. More Stravinsky than Gershwin.

"Come on, Len," JB shouted. "I know you're in there. I can hear you. Up and at em'." He pounded harder on the door.

Finally the door was opened and a sloe-eyed Len stood in the doorway in an open robe and his Calvin Kline briefs.

JB, for a passing moment, took an appraisal of the nearly naked man standing in front of him. Len was, by most people's reckoning, a damned handsome man. He was similar to those Osmond siblings theme song; he was a little bit Tom Selleck and a little bit Richard Gere. Much of it was in the eyes. They were dark and deep with gold flecks that caught the light, speaking of depths that weren't always obvious on a first meeting. That slight cleft in his chin didn't hurt either. It was completely understandable why JB, on first meeting him years before, had fallen so hard. Their brief affair had burned hot and bright for a moment, then fizzled out amongst the ruins of Len's excessive drinking. AA had helped solve that problem and the two men had lately settled into the friendship that now continued between them. Len, in reality, was JB's closest friend and probably the longest running relationship in his life, save for his family back in Kansas.

Len still retained much of his youthful looks—even if both of them were quickly sliding into their mid forties. Len had a well built but untoned body—visits to the gymnasium were looking like they might be necessary in the near future—especially since hard body muscled looks were becoming so popular among the denizens of their gay world. JB, on the other hand, was more the long and lean type. Taller than Len by two inches he was all elbows and knees, legs and arms. Even now he still had some of the adolescent gangleyness that had plagued his youth. His sedentary working conditions as a writer were leading to a just becoming noticeable potbelly. The gym looked to be in JB's future also.

Len's hair, once a deep red, was now gone completely gray. It gave him a cosmopolitan look that would almost certainly extend his acting career by playing patriarchs, bank presidents, and the like. JB had touches of gray at the sides of his own dirty blond hair that hopefully put one in mind of the hot daddy type, which was a selling point for a goodly number of the gay population.

Len closed his robe and cinched the belt. "This is not funny, JB. I was in the middle of a really lovely dream...lots of good looking men...and here you've gone and screwed it up. When I'm the one who was going to be doing the screwing. Fah." He made a sour face.

"Oh dear, somebody sure woke up on the wrong side of David Hasselhoff this morning. Get something on. We have to get to the police station. Now."

"You're being a regular Miss Pushy this morning, aren't you? I have to get dressed, for God's sake. You can't expect me to be seen in public looking like this..."

"Isn't that what I just said? Besides half the male population of Charlies bar on a Saturday night has seen you in far less than that. Go get dressed..."

JB took a seat at the kitchen table, grabbed the entertainment section of last Sunday's Times and began to read. Finishing that, he next started on the Style section, then the Metro section, and then the twelve page Magazine. He was still waiting.

JB had sat there while Len went about his morning ablutions. Len had hot showered, cold showered, body washed and moisturized, almond scrubbed and avocado masked, mango conditioned and apricot depilated. The man was a virtual Carmen Miranda of beauty products. Then he'd moussed, airwaved, gelled and exfoliated, bronzed and brushed, plucked and chaffed. Obviously still looking youthful took a great deal of work on his part. JB was about ready to chew his knuckles off.

Next came the day's wardrobe. Would it be casual or more formally suited? Armani or Hugo Boss? Maybe

Calvin Klein? Shirt: Perry Ellis or Bill Blass? A stripe or a solid? Button down or clipped. Pointed or rounded collar? Shoes: wing tips or the Gucci loafers? Tie: woven or silk? Patterned or striped? Wide or narrow. When Len had trouble deciding what pocket square to use with what tie JB was up to eating dirt and biting rocks.

"For God's sake, Len, will you move your ass. This is ridiculous. Marie Antoinette didn't take this long to get ready for a ball. This male dandy thing has gone way too far."

"I am simply exercising my gay given right to be flamboyant. I want to look my best."

"You know, there'll soon come a day when even your birthday suit will be vintage clothing. It's a losing battle, Len."

Len checked himself in his full length mirror. "I swear, I'm a peacock in a world of pigeons." He swept his hand over his lapel. "Well, come on, what are you waiting for. Let's go. Chop, chop."

※※※

They walked up the steps of the police station a half hour later, after a wild drive to the Village with a Turkish cab driver who had to be mad as hell at someone since he kept up a rambling monologue in a foreign tongue the entire time. His tip came to less than two dollars, which was cause for more angry words. The cab tires burned rubber as it took off.

"Here, put this in your pocket..." JB held out the VCR tape from the bookstore. "Practice those pickpocketing skills you were bragging about and leave this somewhere where the cops will be sure to find it."

Len took it and unbuttoned his coat. The tape fit nicely into the inner breast pocket. Len huffed, "Do I have to? It really ruins the line of the jacket. It makes it all lumpy."

"You won't have it all that long. And *Women's Wear Daily* won't fault you since its in a good cause."

※※※

The reception desk was straight ahead, a long

slab of processed wood with Plexiglas panels attached to the top and rising to the ceiling. Behind the glass sat a youngish man in uniform. JB bent to talk at the circle of holes drilled in the glass so he could be heard, and stated their reason for being there.

The young man picked up a phone, talked into it for a moment, then indicated they should have a seat on a wooden bench over against the lobby wall.

The precinct building was one of those Sixties whitewashed cinder block square shaped modern buildings popular when the city still had money to spend on architecture and architects. Before budget cuts and dwindling reserves made such extravagance impossible. Behind the reception desk was a large open pit broken up with gray fabric standing cubicles, making it feel more like a bank office or a mouse maze than a police station. It was only the uniforms and the occasional flash of a gold badge that made it cop like. Along the outer walls were a series of metal framed windowed offices with fabric vertical blinds running across them to open or close for privacy.

JB sat and pulled a book from his backpack, opened it to its mark, and began to read. Len stayed standing, looking over the layout of the room. He looked down at JB. "Back on the right, there's a kid with a TV monitor and a stack of tapes in front of him. Do you suppose?"

JB didn't look up. "Could be. We can check it out when we're called back."

Which happened about five minutes later. A female cop came over to them, checked their names on her clip board, and then led them down a side aisle toward the back where the homicide squad's office was located. When they passed the cubical Len had spotted from the front he veered off to stop and talk with the occupant. A blond twenty-five year old boy with full lips and soulful eyes.

JB continued following the woman, who took him to an office with gold decal lettering spelling out whose it was on the door. Lieutenant Martin Greenberg. Homicide. She knocked, pushed it open, and gestured him in. Greenberg, sitting behind a pressed wood and chrome utilitarian desk, appeared to be in late middle age—somewhere from the late fifties to retirement. Balding, paunchy, harassed, rumpled. Looking like he hadn't slept in a week or so. Various half empty cups of deli coffee scattered over the cluttered desk attested to the fact.

"I thought there were two of you?" he said appraising JB. He looked over at the woman cop still standing behind JB. "How'd you lose one in the space of fifty feet? For God's sake, find the other one." and he waved her to her task. "Have a seat, Mr...?"

"Bent. Jeremy Bent."

"Okay, Mr. Bent. You have a statement to make, is that correct? On the Weatherwax murder?" He started ruffling through the papers on his overcrowded desk.

"As you requested, Lieutenant."

"Here it is." He grabbed a file. "Sorry about that. This is one of three other killings that same night. In this precinct alone. Not including the rest of New York City. Many more there." He sighed and opened the file folder. "Well, thank you for coming down. I'm not so sure we'll need your statement after all. We've already caught the killer. A Jay Nathan Holt it was..." He read from the file he held.

"Well, that's why I'm here, Lieutenant. I'm not so sure you do have the right man. My friend can provide an alibi for Mr. Holt."

He looked confused. "Friend? An alibi? You're saying the man we have isn't our killer...What are you? Meshuga?"

That's when Len opened the door and walked in. "Okay, okay. You don't have to push..." He was looking back at the lady cop. "So, I'm here. I don't know why you're so upset. It turns out the young man and I are distantly related. His mother and my mother are both mothers. We have a date for Friday..." He sat next to JB.

Greenberg looked to be impressed. A famous somebody had just walked into his office. "You're Len

Matthews, aren't you? I saw your show on Broadway. You were pretty good."

"Why, thank you. Always nice to meet a fan."

"This is the friend I mentioned, Lieutenant. He'll give your suspect an alibi for the time of the killing."

"That's right, sir. He was with me. At my apartment. Clear up on the East Side at the time of the killing."

Greenberg leaned back in his chair. "And how do you know when the killing took place?" He looked again at the report in his file. "We only have an approximate..."

"It was around midnight, right? Well, Jathan got to my place at ten-thirty. I got home about fifteen minutes later. He'd brought Chinese. Lo-Main and Moo-Shu Pork with those Chinese pancakes I like so much. We finished eating around eleven-thirty. It was late so Jathan stayed the night. That's how I know he couldn't have done it."

"The murder could have taken place much later than midnight, Mr. Matthews. Did he leave your place anytime during the night?"

"No. It was..." JB kicked at Len's foot, then shook his head slightly when Len looked over. "Oh, well..."

That's when the young cop Len had been seducing stuck his head in the door. He smiled at Len. Greenberg cleared his throat. "Oh, uh, Lieutenant, you need to see something..."

"Not now, come back later."

"But it's important, sir. I found the tape..."

That got his attention. He sat up, saying, "I told you..."

"No, no. It's all right, Lieutenant," JB said. "We'll just wait here for you. You go ahead. Do what you have to do."

Greenberg got up and went with the young man.

JB turned to Len. "You got rid of the tape then?"

"Of course. The hardest part was getting wonder child there to begin looking at it. I had to practically lead him to it like a calf to his mother's teat. He was watching it when that woman came in and dragged me away. But it looks like he figured it out for himself. Clever boy."

JB and Len sat in the Lieutenant's office for about ten minutes, until he came back and sat at his desk. He looked at them. "Well, as I said, it looks like we won't be needing your statements after all. We'll be releasing Mr. Holt momentarily. There are still a few questions we need to ask him."

"Then he isn't your killer?"

"It doesn't appear so. A surveillance tape we located has proved otherwise. You can see Mr. Holt very soon. We're bringing him up right now." He indicated outside his office.

Jathan, wearing the one piece jumpsuit of a prisoner, was being led to an interrogation room. Len got up, left the office, and went to intercept him. JB followed. As did the Lieutenant.

"You're okay?"

Jathan gave Len a wan smile. "Tired, but I'll survive. Thank you for coming."

"They'll be letting you go in..." Len looked to the Lieutenant.

"A couple of hours."

"Is there anything we can do?"

"I'll need some clean clothes. Could you get some from my place? Maybe the Lieutenant can give you the key from my personal effects?"

He nodded.

"Sure. Of course, we can do that for you. Can't we JB? And then we'll come back to pick you up later."

"Maybe you could let Suzy know I'm getting out too?"

"You bet."

Chapter 9

LEN TURNED ON the overhead lights in Jathan's loft, then headed for the carved cupboard against the wall by the bed that acted as a closet. JB was more interested in the studio area and headed back there.

"Now don't go snooping around, JB. We're only getting his clothes. Will a pair of jeans and a pullover be all right, do you think? Maybe I should get underwear too?"

"I'm not snooping. It's out in the open for all to see. I just want to check it out."

"What is? What have you latched onto?" He came back to where JB was standing in front of the easel behind Jathan's workbench.

On their first visit to the loft the easel had been covered with a tarp. Now it was uncovered, and held a very nice watercolor and pastel drawing of a white faced dancing clown surrounded by flowers and birds; there was even a rabbit playing a violin to add a touch of whimsy to the whole composition.

Len stood next to JB.

"What do you think?"

"It's nice enough. Not at all like his usual work."

"Do you think it was done by Jathan?"

"It's in his studio, isn't it?"

"But this isn't his style at all. It's more like some other artist. I'm trying to think who. Matisse maybe? Or Picasso? Someone I've seen at the MOMA."

"Too realistic for Picasso."

"True. Wait, I've got it. It's like a Chagall. Have you seen the Metropolitan Opera ceiling he painted? Same style as this."

"You don't suppose it's real do you?"

"Does Jathan have enough money to afford a real Chagall?"

"A reproduction maybe."

"But this isn't a print." JB bent down to look closer at the little drawing. "There's none of those little dots you get with a print. I think this is the real deal. It might be a sketch or a maquette from the Met project. Since Chagall died a couple of years ago any of his works are becoming pricey. Even remnants."

"Maybe Jathan bought it before Chagall died. When it was still cheap."

"Except that Chagall has never been that cheap. His oil paintings sold in the tens of thousands even when he was still alive. God knows what they're worth now. What a drawing this size would go for I'm not sure. A couple of thousand I'd bet. You know, I think I need to find that out. What this is worth, I mean."

Len was already huffing and puffing. He had nothing on that nursery rhyme character with the pigs. "Now, JB, we've just gotten Jathan off of a murder charge and now you want to start checking out his paintings? You can't suspect him of something? You can't, damn it."

"I wish I had my camera. I could take a picture of this and show it to someone..."

"Who would you show it too? Come on, its just a little drawing with a few paint dabs. Maybe Jathan did it himself. Artists copy other artists don't they? It's sort of standard practice, right?"

JB had to agree. "When they're students an artist will copy, sure. But eventually they all aim to have their own style, not copy somebody else's. Even writers do it. My first stories all sounded like bad Raymond Chandler. Len, I know you like Jathan, but don't let it turn your head. Wait, I think I saw a deli on the corner. Maybe you..."

"I could what?...I ask you trepidaciously."

"Is that even a word?"

"No. It's a feeling, and I don't like it."

"What I was going to ask is if you would go down to the deli and buy one of those disposable cameras. That way we could take pictures of the sketch and Jathan would never be the wiser. He'd never even know we're looking into it."

"What you mean *we*, kemo-sabe?" Len said, repeating JB's jab from earlier. JB stared him down. Len caved.

"Okay, I'll get the camera, but that's as far as my involvement will go." He pushed the clothes he was holding into JB's arms and headed for the door.

JB set the clothes down on the worktable and continued with his inspection of Jathan's studio. He was perfectly aware that snooping was a bad habit of his, and could even be considered illegal by some of the more narrow minded of his acquaintance. But it was also the only way JB could satisfy the instincts and alarms that kicked in when something didn't feel right about a given situation. And there was something about this whole thing that was feeling very wonky to him right then.

For one thing, how did Jathan get involved in all this in the first place? Some stranger hires him to paint a display window? He just calls, from out of nowhere, and offers a job that pays a hungry artist a huge amount of money? What kind of budget does this bookstore have anyway? Gongs were pealing. Bells were tinkling.

And another think...Who the hell was Weatherwax to begin with? And what possible motive was there for him being killed? Some look-a-like of a rising artist walks into a display window, has an argument with the man, and knifes him in the gut? Why? Horns blaring. Chimes dinging.

And now there arrives this little picture mystery. Here we have a famous artists work, albeit a small rather insignificant drawing, sitting on an easel in a starving artists home? Well, maybe Jathan's not starving exactly, but he's struggling for sure. JB looked around. The loft, although not posh, wasn't exactly a garret out of a Dickens novel. There had to be some money coming in from somewhere? Advertising work as he had claimed? Or Starzy's largess? Or was it maybe something more sinister? Something more fraudulent? Triangles tinging. Knockers clacking.

Was the little Chagall drawing part of Jathan's personal art collection? Or was it something a tiny bit more than that? Was it fraud? A fake? Whistles shrilling. Semaphore flags waving.

JB turned back to the drawing to check again if it might be real. He looked closely at each of the corners. Then at the whole piece. He noticed it wasn't signed.

If it was a sketch cut from a larger work of Chagall's that might be a good reason for it not to be signed. Or? If it's only a copy by Jathan, as Len insisted, there might not be a signature? Or? Or? Any one of those two reasons could explain why the painting wasn't signed. Maybe that's a yet? The name would come later? As JB understood it, a forgery isn't called a forgery until it has a false signature applied to it.

What would be the scenario then? Jathan's a poor artist. He's in need of money. Aren't we all? How much money? Art forgery can earn thousands of dollars at a crack. One little fake Chagall would get him those thousands wouldn't it? After all, Jathan certainly wouldn't be the first talent to turn to fakery to make a living. Was that how the bookstore manager Weatherwax was involved in this? Was he the dealer?

Here they come JB realized. That long list of questions that he wanted the answers to before he could let this go. Before the whole affair would stop niggling at him. Would stop waking him up in the middle of the night.

Putting the questions aside for the moment, JB went over to the wall where the racks of Jathan's paintings were stored. He stood on tiptoe and flipped through them, one after another. What he found was more of Jathan's male dominated illustration like paintings. Over a hundred hunky men standing in a row. How nice it must be to work in a profession where you get to paint gorgeous men's bums all day, every day. Did Jathan use models?

In the entire rack JB didn't find another artist did one other work that looked like it. But even that could be considered cause for suspicion. If Jathan was collecting other artists, like Chagall, wouldn't there be at least one work by another artist somewhere around? Only Jathan's own art was displayed in the loft, whether it was framed and hung in the living area or stored in the bins. It was that little Chagall that was the anomaly. It didn't belong. Then what was it doing here?

JB spotted a cabinet at the other end of the racks. It was a stack of narrow drawers ten or twelve high on a metal stand. The kind of cabinet architects, or artists, use to store blueprints and sketches. JB opened the top drawer and found exactly that. Sketches. Jathan's sketches. Preliminary drawings for more ambitious works Jathan might be planning. The next drawer was more of the same.

It was the third drawer that stopped JB cold. Because in it was another Chagall. A Chagall that looked exactly the same as the one on the easel—a white face clown and a violin playing rabbit. Perhaps it was a practice piece for that final copy? And under that one was another drawing. This one looked like a Miro. At least it seemed to have the artists usual clean sharp lines. It also was unsigned. Another copy? Another practice piece soon to be a forgery? By now fire alarm bells were clanging in his head loud enough to wake the dead.

Len returned with a bottle of *Snapple* tea for each of them and handed over the rectangular cardboard box that held a roll of thirty-five millimeter film. Called a *Quick-Snap* by the Fuji company, it had been introduced just the year before. These throw-away cameras were meant to be cheap and convenient and for outdoor tourist type photography, however it would also serve JB's needs. JB retrieved a floor lamp and placed it near the drawing to make it brighter for the lens. Then standing a few feet back he took twelve or so pictures of the little drawing.

"I'll show these to a friend and see what's what?"

Len chided him. "What you *suspect*, you mean. I hate it when you go into one of these ace detective modes of yours." He opened the bottle of tea and took a swig. JB could tell he was going to go on one of his tirades so he probably needed the nourishment. He started pacing, revving up for what he had to say. JB tried not to pay attention. Ignoring Len was sometimes the only defense. It wouldn't serve to stop him though.

"You are really something, fellow." Len pointed a finger. "When did you get to be so damned suspicious, JB? So cynical? Do you trust anyone anymore? I mean, seriously?" Len swung his arms, splashing a bit from his open tea bottle onto the floor. He spun around. "There is absolutely nothing here that I can see that would make me think that Jathan is involved in any sort of criminal activity. Nothing" JB came around to where Len was pacing as Len stopped his spin and crossed his arms. "Yet here you are, taking pictures, looking in corners, peeking under rocks."

JB took Len's tea from his hand and set in the workbench. "Watch what your doing, Len. You're splashing that tea all over."

"It isn't a pretty trait, JB. You know what? I think you need help my friend. Professional help."

JB bent to look at the easel. "Well, the livelihood I've made out of these suspicions of mine will more than pay for any therapy you say I need." He stood straight up and pointed. "Now look at what you've done, Len. There's wet tea marks on the bottom of this drawing." He picked up a rag from the table and dabbed at the spots left from Len's energetic diatribe. "That's going to leave a stain."

Len came over to stand with JB. "Do you think Jathan will notice? Did I ruin it?"

"The spots are tiny. Hopefully he won't notice them. But be careful with that bottle. And for your information, no matter what you may think, my crazy suspicions about things have led me to the plots for several books so far. You know I'm crazy about solving puzzles. This is just another one of them. So I'm not going to knock it. And maybe you shouldn't either."

Len held up both his hands. "I'm just saying..."

"And if you want something that will raise even your suspicions take a look in that cabinet over there. Maybe that will convince you I'm not so wrong." Len looked at him strangely, then went to the cabinet. He started opening the drawers.

"What I'm saying, Len, is that there's something not right about all this."

Len turned back to face JB. He had found the second Chagall and the Miro. "Okay, I'll give you that there's no reasonable explanation for these. But I still prefer to think Jathan is just copying for his own use."

"Believe what you will, but I think we need to look into exactly who John Weatherwax was. What was his involvement in all of this."

"And what about Starzy? Shouldn't you look into her too?"

"As a matter of fact..."

"And how about Mother Teresa while you're at it? Or the Queen Mother?"

"Len. Stop it. I get your point, but I really don't want to hear it."

"You know if you really only want to hear what *you* want to hear you'll need to take up ventriloquism."

"Keep it up, Len, and I swear I'll put fishhooks in your nipples and fly you off the Chrysler building as a flag."

"Now that's kinky."

Chapter 10

WHERE SHOULD HE start? It wasn't as if JB was a professional investigator with a cortège of informants and stoolies he could contact to find out whatever he needed to know about John Weatherwax, the now dead manager of a local gay bookstore. To be honest those six novels JB had been bragging to Len about involved a lot of dumb luck and some damn good guessing on his part. He could easily have found himself in the embarrassing position of apologizing for jumping to wrong conclusions on any one of them. But he wasn't going to admit that to Len—he was barely willing to admit it to himself.

So, going back to his original question, where the hell was he going to start looking for information on John Weatherwax? His usual haunts of the New York Public Library or city records both seemed unlikely to yield much, if any, information.

Weatherwax had only arrived in New York a few weeks before, and most likely wouldn't have owned property in the city. Unless he was very wealthy and could afford the exorbitant prices residents paid for their apartments. That seemed unlikely considering his position as a bookstore manager. Though the job would have put him mid-ladder, he wasn't in the Donald Trump category by any means. That made city records useless.

Weatherwax was even less likely to have a reason to be listed in any books published in the last twenty years. Any national scandals concerning him would probably have crossed JB's radar and his name would have been more familiar. That cut out the newspaper morgue or the library as a source.

Police records were closed to JB as a civilian, so even a minor jaywalking conviction couldn't be rooted out. The cops who were currently handling the case didn't seem liable to hand over any of the information they had so where was he to go?

He kept thinking. An idea started to form. Switches flipped. Lights went on. Chandeliers brightly shone.

Logic dictated that the people Weatherwax worked with should know some bit of gossip about the man. Even on the short acquaintance they had of him they probably knew something JB didn't. They would have some tidbit that might take JB to the next step. That called for a return to the bookstore where Weatherwax had worked.

After stopping at a one hour photo store to have the Chagall drawing pictures he'd taken developed

JB found himself walking into the front entrance of *A Different Read*, Weatherwax's bookstore.

Thank the heavens for gay bookstores. They were the wellspring of knowledge about gay lifestyles for us all. They provided, over the past twenty years or so, if nothing else proof to us that we existed. A questioning youth could find answers in them. An isolated man or woman could find others of his kind in them. Militants found flyers on upcoming protests in them. Gays could find entertainment and pride and information in them. Most larger cities had at least one alternate bookstore to provide a place for our kind. New York had at least five or six, including *A Different Read*, along with all the straight bookstores that had finally realized we were a market and started providing a good sized section of gay and lesbian literature on their shelves.

A Different Read pretended it was an independent family owned cozy old fashioned book business, but it was in reality only a cog in the wheels of a larger conglomerate of gay owned businesses based out of offices located in the Empire State Building over in Midtown. The business model was rooted in the big brother corporate practice of absorbing other companies and gathering them all under one rainbow colored umbrella. It was a sort of fey Procter and Gamble. This particular aggregate included an S&M bar named *The Tool Box*, a porn movie studio called *Wild Bull Productions*, *Throb Publishing*, which put out skin mags and stroke books. And the bookstore, of course. All were cozily clustered under a queen mother company called *Iron Eagle Ltd*. Amazing what you could find out if you took the time to read little brass plaques by entrances and then checked phone book listings under *Corporations*.

The conglomerate was also the reason JB found the assistant manager who had unveiled Weatherwax's body had not been promoted to manager of the store after the death of his boss. His place in the wheels of the business was fixed no movement forward or up allowed. There was a new manager running the store now. And a more puffed up corporate stooge he couldn't have been. Both as pious and snooty as a backwater Boston minister he had no idea about who or where John Weatherwax had even come from. Do you know the word unhelpful?

Also, as if to further prove the new broom effect, the Jathan painted backdrop in the window had been removed. Whether that was by the police as evidence or by the new manager's obvious disdain for the work wasn't clear. Also the outsider book display meant to make the place hipper had been replaced with a boring collection of travel guides. Gay Florida. Queer Quebec. The business of selling would never be interrupted by something so lowly as a murder.

JB walked the bookstores aisles until he found the assistant manager he had met the day of the murder. He was busy restocking the gift card racks. He continued to place cards while they spoke.

"I liked John. He wasn't one of these corporate toadies that we usually get around here. He was nice to us." Thus giving his opinion of both the new manager and John Weatherwax in one fell swoop. Unfortunately, the boy had a tendency to nasality when he spoke, plus he hailed from the Bronx, so there was a double whammy in listening to him. "But he was from out on the West Coast so that's probably the reason. People are cooler out there, ya know what I mean? John had dropped everything to come here and work (Pronounced *woik*.). He said he couldn't pass up a chance to take on da Big Apple."

"Then how long had he been here?"

"Just a while. A month, maybe a month and a half. Him and his Sweets."

"Sweets? Is that a boyfriend?"

"Naw, its a dog. He doted on it."

"He had a dog named Sweets?"

"John said it was a shorter version of Sweetdarlingcutiepie. A poodle dachshund mix. Ugliest animal you ever did see. A hairy hotdog with a poufy tuft of a tail and a bow on its head. But John loved the little thing." This guy was obviously not a dog person.

"How about a partner? Did he have one of those too?"

"Naw, I don't think so. He never mentioned one if he did. But actually (Pronounced *axely*) there were rumors Mr. Bevan was the one he was after. John had a little crush on him."

"Bevan?"

"Bevan Jones. The CEO of the company that owns this place. John was brought here by him and made manager right off. He didn't even have to work his way up. Lucky queen. John was supposed to have some radical ideas for the store. That's what the painting in the window was all about. He was going for something groovier for the store."

"Which didn't go over so well, I guess. Since the painting has been removed."

"It had blood stains on it, but you're right. This new manager hated it." He looked around as if he had a piece of dirt he couldn't say outloud. JB was intrigued enough to lean in. "To be honest, I don't think I'm going to stay in this dump. I'm looking for something else. Say, I helped you here, didn't I? Maybe you'll help me now? Any ideas?"

Sigh. JB would never get used to it. Everybody seemed to always be working a deal. Washing other peoples backs for favors was a way of life in the city. JB thanked him, and since the kid really had helped, handed over a business card from his publisher. "Maybe there's a job there," he told him. "Use my name if you want, although I don't guarantee it will help."

JB left the store then. He was aiming for the corporate offices and the CEO of *Iron Eagle Ltd.* That was how these things seemed to work for him. Like a children's party treasure hunt. Pick up a sting and follow it under bushes and around trees until it led you to the prize at the end. The assistant had provided a string for JB to follow. He would go where it took him. He had his start.

JB would head to midtown and the Empire State Building, but not before he picked up the pictures of the drawing from the photo place. He already knew where he was taking those. It was another string to follow.

※ ※ ※

The sidewalks of Midtown that time of day were the precise definition of the word frenzy. Lunchtime crowds surged and pushed like swarms of killer bees along every street. People were crowded together like tuna in a school. Getting to the polished brass deco doors of the Empire State Building was an exercise in urban survival. Go straight forward, don't give way, make a space for yourself, forget your manners, ignore any untoward gropes from strange hands.

The building's lobby was an Art Deco jewel, polished and gleaming with Thirties glamour; striated marble floors and walls, linear style decorations picking out the vaulted ceilings. Gold relief carved elevator doors opened and closed once they filled with tourists heading for the eighty-second floor observation deck above the city, with magnificent three hundred and sixty degree views. The next crowd was ganged up in front of the main bank of cars, waiting for the uniformed guide to open the doors for their ascent.

JB walked away and took one of the other elevators. The car doors closed and it began going up. Which set off that slight fear of heights that plagued him in the city. A stupid phobia to have in a world populated with soaring skyscrapers, but there he was. Afflicted. He coped by staying away from windows that looked straight down and by always avoiding balconies.

The lobby board listing the building's occupants had indicated that *Iron Eagle Ltd.* had a suite on the thirty-fifth floor. The elevator took him up swiftly, then opened onto a silent hallway. Painted numbers and arrows on the wall pointed JB in the direction he needed to go.

The hallway was what you often saw in Nineteen thirties built buildings, plain painted plaster with brown wood wainscoting at waist height, broken occasionally by pebbled glass and metal doors—except it all had a shabby aged feel from the preceding fifty years of wear. Old New York was like that. It often seemed to be wearing a fur coat with no panties. It could be all glitz on the outside, while a bit tired behind the facade.

JB turned a corner and saw the double doors of *Iron Eagle Ltd.* directly ahead. A dark metallic relief casting of the company logo—which was an angry bald bird with lightning bolts clutched in its talons—was hung on the center with raised old English lettering spelling out the name below. JB opened the door, which split the eagle in half.

The door led into a reception outer office which at that moment was empty. Decorated in the style of an English barrister's rooms it appeared to be simply an elaborate stage set. If JB was pushed for an opinion he would guess it was meant to make an impression of stability and solidity. Stretching for respectability. What really came across was stiff, stodgy and mildly oppressive. It reeked of upper class pretensions run amuck. But then, according to the research JB had been able to accomplish, mainly gossip from his assistant manager friend at the bookstore, the company was owned by a pornmonger seeking some kind of estimable status. If that was so, the decor could be expected.

The walls, veneered with panels of enough precious wood to endanger an Amazon rainforest, were hung with several ornate gold framed oil paintings. Good ones from what JB could tell. The owner had some taste in art at least. The works consisted of Eighteenth and Nineteenth century rococo landscapes, a couple of riding to hounds panorama's, and a few long dead aristocrats with disapproving eyes looking upon those beneath them. The paintings were hung from woven tasseled cords going up to the fake cornice that outlined the sham coved ceiling. An antique carved desk stood over on the far wall; an overstuffed red leather couch and chair sat on the other. It was all very Queen Anne, very Laura Ashley, very la-tee-da, don't ya know. But what JB wondered was where the hell the people were? It was an office after all. A place of business. He'd waited several minutes and there was no sign of another human.

Then he heard what sounded like a moan coming from behind the dark oak door at the side of the desk. He crossed to it and listened closer. He heard another moan. Somebody in that other room was hurt? He put his ear closer. When there came yet another moan he decided he'd better go in. Someone might be injured. He grabbed the knob and pushed.

Inside, at another monstrosity of a desk sat a middle-aged man. Forty-five, maybe closer to fifty. On first impression he was rugged, manly, like one of the models in the magazine cigarette ads you saw every month. He had impeccably dyed and groomed brown hair, with a strong face that was beginning to sag slightly around the edges. He wore a starched white shirt with a designer tie slung over one shoulder. His head was thrown back and his eyes were closed as if in a daze. JB wasn't sure if it was from pain or from passion.

At the sound of JB entering the man's head jerked up, surprise coloring his face. His eyes opened, and he looked over at JB with one of those "what the hell" expressions. Then another man's head rose up from the floor in front of him. Younger by probably thirty years and impossibly cute in that way only twenty something twinks can manage, his own natural brown hair was mussed and his face was flushed a cupid pink. His eyes got big, and then he grinned the knowing grin of the sexually promiscuous. He raised a hand and motioned an invitation for JB to join them.

Ah ha. It was passion then. Sex had been the reason for the moans JB had heard. The older man, still in his chair, put a hand on the boy's head and pushed it back down into his crotch. Then he looked over at JB, smiled a little guiltily, and raised his hand in a come on and join gesture of his own.

"Quite all right," JB demurred. "I'll just wait out in the front. You'll be what?" He looked at his watch. "A minute or three more?" He backed out and closed the door.

Well, so what? It happened all the time. In

every office. In every building. All over New York City. Afternoon delights. Happy endings. Getting laid. Straight or gay. Malcolm Forbes and his male clerks. Donald Trump and his chorus girl girlfriend. BJ's or FU's. Business men of all persuasions were notorious for their sexual rapacity. As long as both parties were willing and a line wasn't crossed to a sexual predator situation then it wasn't a problem. When it became harassment and power wielding by one party against another then it just wasn't acceptable. But a gay man in the porn business? Well, hold the door open, Nellie.

A few minutes later the young man came out of the office and smiled at JB snidely. "You should have stayed. It might have gotten you what you're here for a lot faster." He obviously wasn't being forced into what JB had seen. He also had to be assuming that JB was a salesman on a call. The boy sat at his desk and examined his nails. "It's always worked for me." Which one of the two participants was the predator here?

JB looked him up and down. So young to be so snappish. Another nascent bitchy queen. That sort of attitude would be guaranteed to bring out JB's more evil side. "You know," he said looking down his own nose at the pretentious baby queen, "you really shouldn't talk. It's canceling out all the hard work your ass has been doing."

Miss Snidely waved a limp hand in bored dismissal. "Go on in. Mr. Jones will see you now."

JB started for the office door, then stopped. Another comment probably wouldn't help any, but why pass up the chance? The line was already in the breech, right? So fire away..."I'm pretty sure you've been called bitch more often than a new prisoner on Rikers Island. Well, guess what? They're right."

He opened the door and stepped in.

※※※

"To put your mind at ease, Mr. Jones. I have nothing to sell you."

JB in his first moments checked out the office. The decor of a man's office can offer much useful information about its owner. Clues to his likes and dislikes — is he into modern or traditional, chic or tacky. Or does he have someone that does the decorating for him. This room didn't have any obvious decorator touches. Plain, if not almost austere, it looked to be completely its owners personal taste. The upper class English veneer of the front was absent here. This was a modern beige room with a large uncurtained window at its end to fill it with light. The walls were covered with a satin finished paper that served as background for more pieces from the man's art collection lined along the walls. Each similarly framed, there were abstracts, moderns, and impressionists instead of the more traditional works he'd seen out front. There was a Courbet oil, a Modiglani lady, a Matisse, and a few lesser known works. All of which gave the room a Madison Avenue gallery feel. If the art was real — and JB suspected they were — it was a nice enough collection for anyone to boast about.

Jones stood up behind his desk. "I wouldn't say that, Mr...? I'm sorry, I don't know your name, but you look like you have a few assets that could get a pretty good price." He sounded like syrup poured on a waffle while he lecherously looked JB up and down.

Good God, sexual innuendo? Even after just finishing up with the baby bitch out front? Give it a rest, fella.

"And from the collection of art you have here you would know about value wouldn't you? But thanks for the compliment. No, what I mean is I'm not a salesman. I've come to ask some questions. About one of your employees. Or rather an ex-employee. Oh, and my name is Jeremy Bent." He held out his hand.

Now that the man was sans his suckor JB could appraise him better. As first believed Bevan Jones was handsome in that Old Spice ex-jock sort of way that would appeal to ninety-five percent of the gay population. Strong jaw, slight five o'clock shadow, bushy brows over deep dark ironic seeming eyes. Make that one hundred and five percent of the gay population. When younger he had to have been the prettiest man at the bar. The one everyone wanted to lay. Now, in his late forties, he maybe had to work a little harder, but JB was sure he still got what he wanted. And being a player in the gay pornography business it was probably a hell of a lot. Do the word Satyr ring a bell?

"Bent, huh? And are you bent, Mr. Bent?" As if JB hadn't heard that particular bon-mot a thousand times. "I like you already. And you should call me Bevan." He smiled. "But your name is familiar. Why? Are you famous? Should I know you?"

"Only as a name you might have heard in passing. I'm a writer."

"Oh, well, sorry, I'm not hiring right now." He sat down preparing to get back to work. "I have all the writers I need." JB had been dismissed.

"You mean for those cheap porno paperbacks you sell out of your publishing company? 'Guaranteed to make you Throb...' That's your motto isn't it? That sort of writing is no where near my alley. No, when I write I write mystery novels. And do pretty well with them if I must say."

"Of course. Now I know who you are. Sorry, I didn't mean to offend. Say, I've got something that will really interest you. Come with me."

JB by now had a good idea of why Bevan Jones was so successful in his business. He was one of those men able to make a stranger feel like a close friend in only the first few seconds of their meeting. He simply assumed an intimacy existed between you and worked from there. It could make most anyone feel special. Make them feel as if one of the chosen. And could also cover all sorts of wheeling and dealing in his business matters. JB bet the man could pick a bishop's pocket and not feel the need to confess it.

He stepped out from behind his desk and JB could see that office casual was the apparel of the day. In addition to the white shirt and tie Jones was wearing a pair of button fly jeans and black high tops. The jeans were worn and faded with slits at the knees, the white strings of fabric still hanging. There was something aggressive, sexy, and appealing about the look. Bare knees showing, denim clinging at his thighs and crotch, starched white shirt draped over a well built chest...

JB shook his head to get it back on track. "Uh, the questions I had?"

"Sure, go ahead and ask. I can answer while we walk." He led JB out into the hall, made a turn, and headed down the hallway.

"I was going to ask about John Weatherwax. The man who was killed at your bookstore in the Village."

Bevan stopped walking and turned to JB. "It was tragic what happened to him. And I feel like I'm responsible."

"How is that?"

"I was the reason John was working at the bookstore. I was the one that brought him here from California and gave him the job. If he hadn't moved here..."

"Hardly your fault. You shouldn't feel any blame. Also, I know for a fact the police have a video of the real killer. It's just a matter of time before they find him. How was it you met Mr. Weatherwax?"

"I was in California to visit the new Getty in Malibu. Beautiful, you know? Fine collection, if not sparse. But it is just opened. John was the manager of the gift store. And it turned out he was also a collector like myself. He was selling a piece from his own collection and that's how we were introduced. Through a mutual acquaintance. I liked what I saw in John the first time I met him. Good business head. So, after our dealings were done, I offered him a job."

"Dealings? Then you bought some art from him?"

Bevan started walking again. JB had to step lively to catch up.

"That's right," he said. "A sweet little Chagall sketch. I was going to hang it in my office here, but the shop where I was having it framed was robbed, and that was one of the pieces taken. I'm hoping my security guys can get it back for me. We have had a ransom demand from the thieves. It's being negotiated by my boys now."

"You have your own security team, do you?" Bevan nodded. "And with NYC homicide involved in looking into Weatherwax's death you've got lots of dealings with the law, right?"

Bevan made a yuck face and shrugged.

JB asked, "Is your team taking care of the personal aspects of the case too? For instance, are they contacting Weatherwax's next of kin? For that matter, does he have any kin? A lover maybe?"

"I suppose they are. I'm not sure if he does have any relatives. He must have some family somewhere. Now a partner..." He shook his head. "There was someone he moved here with, but I never met him. We weren't all that close, you understand. I do know he had a dog. He showed me pictures. Mangy looking thing."

"What's happened to the animal I wonder? Has anyone been to his place and checked on it?"

"Good question. I'll call my HR office and check. They'll know better than I would."

"Do you think you could get his apartment address from them too. I'm willing to go and check-up on the animal. If no one has yet. The poor thing must be hungry. I could feed him at least."

Bevan stopped at a door and grabbed the knob. The door's glass insert had the words Throb Publishing painted on it. "This is what I wanted to show you." He opened the door. "Behold the future of writing," he said with a dramatic sweep of his arm.

Inside were two suites of office rooms opened into one. At the front, where JB and Bevan were standing, were several desks holding CRT screens with keyboards. At the back, behind a thick glass wall with sliding doors, were two enormous ceiling tall hulking black machines. Two computer servers with their blinking lights flashing invitingly.

"That back area is air conditioned so the units don't overheat, but take a look at this..."

Bevan went over to one of the desks where a single

young man sat working at his screen. It appeared he was the only human in the room. The entire staff of Throb Publishing?

"What are you doing here?" Bevan asked him.

"Its called 'Butch Men's Prison Orgy'. I'm about half way through."

Bevan looked back at JB and said, "This is so cool. Come on, take a look."

JB moved up to the desk. Bevan was as eager as a boy telling JB about this new toy of his.

"What happens is the computer has been loaded with the plots and the sex scenes from all the books Iron Eagle has ever published. There are hundreds of them..."

He was right. *Iron Eagle Ltd.* through *Throb* published many of the pulp skin books that sat on racks in the sex shops around Times Square. With titles like "Boys For Sale" and "College Hunk Sex Orgy" they weren't exactly great literature. In fact, they were barely readable.

Bevan went on, excited by the idea he was presenting to JB. "...then all my CRT guy here has to do is put what he wants for the book he's working on into the search function and the computer pulls everything that relates to that subject up on the screen. In seconds. You make a few sentence adjustments and, zingo, you have a new book." He turned back to the clerk. "Go ahead, type fellatio into search." The man did so. In less than a minute the computer started showing sets of sentences and paragraphs concerning that particular sex act. "See. All this guy has to do now is read through those and use whichever one's apply to the book he's working on. He can do two, sometimes three, new books a day." Bevan was puffed with pride at what his computer tech guys had wrought.

JB was, to put it mildly, horrified. "You mean to say this thing...this computer has mechanized writing to where an actual writer isn't even needed? You're saying you only need a collator. That the creative genius of Charles Dickens, Victor Hugo, or even Stephen King should be discarded for the work of a...a...file clerk?"

"Yep. Isn't it great."

JB almost gagged on his actual opinion of this outright bastardization of his life's work. He could remember times when it took an hour to mould a sentence to mean exactly what he wanted it to mean, of days spent finding the true meaning of a paragraph. And this yahoo wanted to make all of that meaningless? And you wonder why people find themselves able to kill. To JB the English language was a sort of musical, magical mixing of sounds. He would even get a linguistic stiffy at times from their effects. It was the idea of words and what they can do. What a person can do with the words, and what words can do to each other. Maybe the coming computer age everyone is so hot about isn't such a terrific thing after all. Change the world? Maybe. Make all art obsolete? Disaster.

Bevan didn't even notice JB's distress. "Although these skin books aren't selling all that great anymore," he went on. "VCR's are making them obsolete nowadays. People would much rather watch it than have to read about it. I don't know how much longer we'll even publish these."

"Well, that's a relief. The whole idea is unspeakably terrifying, I must say."

Bevan made no notice and instead was going on about his video business. How it made up at least ninety percent of his profits now. "VCR's have revolutionized the porn business in the last few years. Gay and straight porn. It was all growing huge. You should excuse the pun." He chuckled at his limp joke. Then he went on to say he had a studio in a building downtown where he turned out a movie a week.

"What about the AIDS crisis? Hasn't the disease affected the porn business some?"

"Not really. Except to make it bigger. Porn has to be the ultimate in safe sex, right? Lately we've been made to use condoms for the actors. It's now an industry standard. But that's a minor inconvenience. We use pink colored rubbers and you hardly notice them on film."

They were walking back to Bevan's office. "Say," he asked. "maybe we could go out sometime? You and I. How about dinner?"

They stopped in front of the door to *Iron Eagle Ltd.*

"You mean go out together?" JB marveled at how easily Jones made asking for a date seem. In the last several years the way gay men met each other had gone through a titanic change. In the old days of the sexual revolution you cruised, you had sex, then you found out names and got to know each other, or you didn't. It could have gone either way. That was part of the joy of it all. But now, six years into this epidemic there had developed a new phenomenon. Men went out on actual dates, got to know each other, and would maybe have sex after three or four of these often uncomfortable and angst inducing meetings. What on earth did straight people see in all of this?

JB wasn't all that sure he wanted to go out with Bevan Jones in any event. The man wasn't really JB's type. Too much of a jock for his taste. He was attractive, yes, but the attitude and that sureness, the arrogance. All that was a total turn-off. Then again, the man was asking for a date, not a lifetime commitment.

JB reached into his backpack and pulled out one of his business cards. "Give me a call. We can arrange something, I suppose. And do you think I could get that address for John Weatherwax before I leave?"

Chapter 11

JB HADN'T VISITED the Lucan Art Gallery in almost a year. Not since he'd bought a small Toulouse-Lautrec sketch that hung in his hallway at home. But he needed to find out what he could about the Chagall drawing he had seen at Jathan's loft so he'd decided to see the owner of the gallery.

Helmut Lucan was a crook and con man who'd

supposedly gone legit, although a cheetah doesn't really change its spots, now does it? Those spots go all the way down to the skin, my friend. He got away with his various art frauds by mixing the good with the bad on his gallery walls. He would put an exquisite Monet next to a blatantly faked Max Ernst. You had to really be on your toes to know the difference. JB knew Lucan would still have at least one sticky finger on what was going on in the local art circles. What was for sale? Who was selling it? And, most importantly, what was being passed around under various tables around the city?

The gallery itself hadn't changed. It still smacked you in the face with its own particular brand of Madison Avenue stiffback snobbish condemnation. JB stepped inside and immediately felt unworthy to be there. The gallery had once again achieved its goal.

Plush gray carpeting, the one shade off white walls, the lighting that picked out the art hung ever so carefully. It all intimidated the crap out of him. The galleries atmosphere was so off putting JB wondered how the man managed to stay in business. Then, just maybe JB wasn't the type of client Lucan was aiming for. JB actually preferred the more experimental works found down in the Soho art district than the mostly establishment art found on the upper East Side.

A young woman approached him. She was in an Ann Kline suit, wearing sensible two inch heels, and black framed harlequin glasses, with a chin length bob. It was the posture and attitude that gave her away though; she was a haircut away from being a regular habitué of *The Duchess*, the Sheridan Square lesbian bar. What was being called lately a lipstick lesbian. In a flat Wellsley accented uppity voice she asked how she could help him. More intimidation intended, JB was guessing.

Then he asked if Helmut was available. Taken by surprise at his familiarity in using the owner's first name, she stiffly asked for his own name and went off to check. That was after looking her surgically bobbed nose down at him, of course.

For some reason JB never managed to make a sterling

impression in these high hat kind of establishments. Too much of his Midwest sodbuster upbringing still clung to him he guessed. He was often mistaken for a delivery boy when he went into these places. It would give him great pleasure to buy something and then pay cash for it. The looks on the clerks faces when he hauled out a wad of bills and began to peel them off more than made up for the sour attitudes they inevitably gave him.

JB waited for Helmut to appear by walking the perimeter of the gallery and looking over the works displayed. As usual he was showing mostly moderns with an emphasis on the early and post impressionists. There were what looked like one or three really good pieces. There was a Picasso, a Signac, a Degas, and several by more contemporary artists, but they were in the correct style for the galleries mandate.

Soon enough Helmut sidled up to him, almost wringing his hands in anticipation at what JB might buy. Sorry to disappoint, old chum.

"Mr. Bent, what a pleasure. Are you still enjoying that little Lautrec drawing we sold you?"

JB was so taken aback his jaw dropped. Helmut had changed since their last meeting. Drastically. He had to be somewhere in his later sixties but fighting it by tooth and with nail. And also by scalpel it appeared. Sometime in the last year the man had gone in for some work. Too much work in JB's opinion.

His face had been lifted. The skin on his face and neck was pulled so tight that he now resembled something put together like a ransom note. Nothing matched. One ear was even set a smidge higher than the other. At one time the man looked his age, now he didn't even look his species. A couple of more surgeries and he could pass for one of his Picassos. When he spoke nothing moved. Not his jaw. Not his lips. Not his forehead. His eyes didn't blink. JB expected his tongue to flick out at any small bugs flying by.

JB gulped to recover himself and said, "Very much, Helmut. You...ah...look well."

He chuckled. "Thank you. Still fighting the good

fight."

And being raped and pillaged, then left by the side of the road, JB was thinking.

"What can we do for you today? Have you seen something you like?"

"I'm very fond of that Hockney there. What's it called?"

"*Boy In A Shower.* Painted in sixty-three. It's a steal at twenty-five thousand."

And you, Mr. Lucan, are the thief, was JB's first thought. "Uh, not today, Helmut" He reached into his backpack. "Why I came today was to show you these." He pulled out the packet of pictures. "I was wondering if you could tell anything about this piece from these snapshots. Anything at all would help."

Helmut took them and held them close to his eyes. Vanity would forbid his wearing glasses, of course. "Let's see what you have." He shuffled the photos quickly. "Ah, it looks to be a Chagall. One of his later drawings, I should think. A nice one at that. It rings all the right bells. Are you considering buying it?"

"What I'm wondering is if it looks like the real thing to you? Or could it be a forgery?"

"Oh, I couldn't possibly say. Not without seeing it up close. It looks right in these." He fanned the pictures. "Like something done for the Lincoln Center Opera House ceiling. But there have been a goodly number of fakes coming on the market over the years. Especially after Chagall died in eighty-five."

"That's what I meant, Helmut. Have you heard about any fake Chagall's being sold recently? Like in the last few weeks? Has there been any scuttlebutt?"

He shook his head. "Oh, dear, no. Today's forgery market is far too clandestine and secretive for me to know anything about it, Mr. Bent. I am completely out of the fakery business after my last run in with the police.*** I'm a legitimate art dealer now."

***His problems with fake paintings can be found in *Secrets Don't Belong In Closets*, the 1st Bent Mystery.

And Boy George is butch.

"Come on, Helmut. You must keep your fingers in the underground art swill. I'll bet you know the true skinny." He fake punched Helmut on his silk suited shoulder. "Come on, give." JB loved piercing Lucan's veneer of civility. Treating him like a crony would always loosen him up.

He hurumped a bit, but nodded and then warmed to the subject. "There was a man a few years ago. Called himself David Stein. He was selling fake Chagall's by the truckload, and Picassos, and Cocteaus, but he was finally caught and went to Sing-Sing to serve time."

"Well, I'm thinking this bit of fakery is going on right now." He pointed to the snapshots. "I saw that piece in an artist's studio, still on the easel, just this morning."

"You did?" Lucan peered at the pictures again. "Then it's a very good copy, Mr. Bent. If it is a copy. Are you sure it wasn't the real thing?"

"It wasn't signed, so no, I'm not sure at all. That's the reason I brought these pictures to you."

Lucan looked behind him, then stepped in closer to speak into JB's ear. Using an indoor voice he said, "There has been some activity lately. Some sort of con game going around town. I'm not sure what it is though. It's not being run by any of the locals. There was a Miro drawing being used as bait with one of my collectors just a few weeks ago. He brought it in to me for authentication. It was real enough, but the price was far too low. It was being given away. I couldn't guess why the seller wanted so little for it. I advised him not to buy it. I don't know what happened after that."

"And now we have a suspicious Chagall showing up. This is building to something big isn't it? Some sort of art theft ring maybe?"

"It isn't good news I have to agree. I'll certainly be on the look out. We get people walking in here with pictures to sell all the time. It's just so easy, you know? Especially with the moderns. Any forger has all the materials he needs still available to him. He doesn't even have to buy old works and strip them. All he has to do is walk into Pearl Paint and pick up the same canvas or paint used by Pollock, or even Matisse. It's all still out there. Available at discount prices."

"Well, that doesn't help much, Helmut. I mean, I'm grateful for the information, but it brings me no closer to answering my question about the Chagall drawing."

"Sorry. I could call my client and ask him what happened with that Miro. Would that help?"

JB said it would. After all, there had been a Miro drawing at Jathan's studio, hadn't there? Lucan said he would call right away. If Mr. Bent didn't mind waiting?

He didn't, but asked if he could use his phone while he did. JB wanted to call Len and see what he was up to. If he had managed to pick up Jathan at the jail and how it had gone. He was simply trying to keep a finger on the pulse of the events swirling about this case.

Lucan walked JB over to the desk where his assistant was seated and told her to let him use her phone. He then excused himself to make the call he'd promised to make. JB sat at the desk and dialed Len's phone number. While it was ringing he began reading the late edition of the *Daily News* that was sitting on the desk.

One of the headlines read: *Graffiti Artist Arrested in Bookstore Murder,* see page 12. Bless the News's sleazy little muckraking tabloid yellow heart.

The inside page had pictures and articles covering the entire mess. *Artist's Identity Revealed* was one article's lead, and it went on to do just that. Tell exactly who Jathan was. He sure wouldn't be needing that Mexican mask anymore. Another of the articles stated that Jathan was at first considered a suspect in the murder of the bookstore manager, but was seen leaving the police station with the actors Len Matthews and Starzy Hillard that afternoon. It appeared he had been cleared of any charges that he may have been suspected of. The picture accompanying the article had Len with his hand held out at the photographer's lens with both Starzy and Jathan holding coats up to cover their faces.

It was a classic tabloid picture. Adjunct to another article detailing the murder itself was a close-up of the bookstore window with Jathan's bloodstained painting shown clearly in the background. That article ended by stating that there was no suspect now that Jathan had been released.

"Have you seen the papers?" Len asked when he answered his phone.

"I'm reading them now. It's typical. Sensational with the substance of a will-o-wisp. How's Jathan taking it?"

"Actually, really well. He's famous..."

"Notorious might be better."

"Whichever. He's been contacted by a Soho galley to do a one man show, so he's ecstatic right at the moment."

"Where are you?"

"At the loft with Jathan."

Then how was he talking with him? JB then remembered that Len had that new fangeled cell phone he'd bought a couple of months ago. At a humongus cost, mind you. The guy paid over three thousand dollars for it! It was another one of Len's toy's he just had to have. It was a bit of a fetish with Len. He always had to have the latest piece of electronic crapola the manufacture's would come up with. Just the other day he was talking about music CD's and their players. JB had said if they were the last damn innovation the companies would come up with he might consider dumping his vinyl records for one of them. But only then. He felt safe enough that he could hang on to his albums for a while longer.

"Starzy's here too," Len went on. "But I'm going to have to leave soon. I have to get to the theater."

"I've got one more errand to take care of and then I can get down there. I need to talk to Jathan."

"We've ordered Chinese so you can eat when you get here. There'll be plenty."

"I should be there by..." He checked his watch. It was nearing three PM. "...I don't know. Five. Five thirty."

"I'll let them know you're coming. Ta." And he was

gone. JB went back to reading the paper, but he had already covered all of what they had reported about the bookstore crime. He was looking at the comics when Helmut returned from his office.

"It was as I suspected, Mr. Bent. The client didn't follow my advice. He went ahead and purchased the Miro. And three days later it was stolen from him. I think the sellers used the drawing to get into his home and case it for a robbery. He lost several other things too. Such bad luck. You have to be so careful anymore."

"So the man's art is now missing?"

Could the Miro that Jathan had at his studio be that stolen drawing? Is Jathan some sort of cat burglar along with his other suspected activities?

"No," Helmut answered. "There was some good luck attending the affair. The thieves called with a ransom demand the very next day. Once that was paid he got his things back, including the drawing."

"Wait. That sounds very familiar. I just heard about the same thing happening to someone else. The robbery and ransom thing I mean."

"Now that I think about it, it is an old con game. It's been around for eons. Con men call it a fake and bake. The ransom demand is a new twist though. There's probably a crew working the grift in the area. They'll stay around for a few months. Until they feel they've worn out their welcome, or think the cops are on to them, then move on to do it again in some other city."

Well, that lets Jathan off the hook. He's a long time resident of New York City. He's not a transient who will be gone in a week. Maybe he isn't involved in this scam after all? There's a perfectly rational and legal reason for him to have the art work he has. Feeling relieved, JB thanked Hulmut for his help, promised to think about the Hockney, and left the gallery.

He did think about the Hockney. But only long enough to laugh uproariously at Helmut's chutzpah at charging so much for it. He made his way to the West Side and the apartment of John Weatherwax.

Chapter 12

JOHN WEATHERWAX HAD lived on the Upper West Side, on Seventy-second at Columbus Avenue. A nice enough neighborhood, if not turning depressingly yuppified of late. Filled with young urban women wearing their designer sportswear, pushing their designer baby carriage's two abreast, blocking off entire sidewalks with all their natal paraphernalia. Most of the gay people, who had previously made the neighborhood interesting, were moving to other environs. To Chelsea mostly. Gay business' were closing. Main Man was gone. Wildwood had been replaced with a Tommy Hilfiger clothing store. Columbus Avenue was going boutique cute.

Instead of flagging down a cab JB had used the opportunity to take a leisurely walk through his favorite spot in all of New York City. He had gone to Fifth Avenue and entered Central Park to make the cross over from the East Side to the West.

The park had been busy with its usual colorful garland of New York denizens. Rollerskaters, teenagers who should have been in school, a mime or two, old men with paper bags of crumbs for the animals and birds, ladies in hats and gloves crowding the benches to soak up the sun and gossip about their perfect grandchildren. Musicians played guitars, and drums, and saxophones, and even plastic buckets. Dancers tapped and spun, hip-hopped, and salsaed. Couples lay entwined and lazed on the green grass. Bikers passed by on paved roads. Frisbees flew back and forth amid raucous yells. Hacky sacks bounced off of young men's feet. Little children chased and terrorized squirrels and pigeons. It was a full on panorama of humanity at its best and worse and all the gray shades between.

As JB walked he went past the spot where the year before he had spotted actress Katherine Hepburn riding her bike. He loved people watching in the city, and an occasional star sighting gave it a little kick every once in a while. One banner day, two years before, he'd spotted William Hurt getting out of a cab on Fifth Avenue, Donald Trump going into the Plaza Hotel at Fifty-seventh Street, Rod Stewart walking toward him on Columbus Avenue, Gwen Verdon going into a cafe at West Fifty-sixth Street, and Mia Farrow walking with one of her children on Amsterdam Avenue. That was a five-star event. Literally. It gave him way more points than Len for that month as a bonus. The dinner he'd won at Len's expense was quite delicious. Unfortunately he hadn't spotted the unicorn of stars, Garbo yet —a sighting of her was worth seventy-five points — but one lived in hope.

JB passed by the newly restored Bethesda fountain with its red brick patterned surround baking in the sunlight. A photo shoot for one of the fashion magazines was going on, giving a sense of glamour to the already over the top Edwardian water display. A stick thin model wearing a black gown with bright rainbow colored bag clips down the back — to make it fit her for the camera — stood at the center of the attention, with her minions fussing around her like ducklings chasing their mother on the glass smooth lake backdrop behind. A solitary rowboat was the only thing to disturb the placid surface of the lake.

When he hit the recently opened Strawberry Fields — Yoko Ono's tribute to her late husband — he slowed. Somehow, when you were in the circle you felt the sense of reverence that filled the memorial roundel. As usual there were several bunches of flowers left on the black mosaic tile word "Imagine" at the center.

JB came out of the park at Seventy-second and West End, directly across the street from the Dakota Apartments looming over the corner it sits on. Since the movie *Rosemary's Baby* and John Lennon's shooting the place has a somewhat ominous presence on the area. Almost as if there was some sort of malefic juju at work in the building. JB checked the address in the letter given him by Bevan's HR department, then stayed on the same side of the street as the apartments. The black painted gargoyle headed iron fencing running along the front of the building added to that sense of disquiet he felt as he passed. The driveway entrance with its tall curved shadowy alleyway leading to the inner courtyard and the brass guard booth standing beside it didn't help much either. You almost expected a Winkie of OZ to be marching back and forth across the front.

At the other end of the street, on Columbus Avenue, he found a Greek diner but no apartment building. He turned around and went back and then spotted the entrance to the apartments he was looking for tucked in a corner behind the diner's extension built out onto the sidewalk. The entrance featured a deco inspired concrete surround holding a single glass door. Inside was a small mirrored foyer that led to a bilious green linoleum floored lobby a few steps up. The lobby wasn't really decorative in any distinctive fashion and held only a bank of mail boxes on one wall, with a wide expanse of seventies gold veined mirror tiles with a fifties coffee table on the opposite wall. At the back, on the left, was the elevator for the seven story building. It had originally been built in the late twenties as a transient hotel, providing kitchen units with living rooms and separate bedrooms for traveling salesmen and the like. Now it was completely residential with small apartments cut from those original full sized rooms. The little nook that held the elevator doors also had a cubby at its back that served as a tiny office. A left over from when the hotel was still active. Looking out from the Dutch door was the manager of the building.

 He was an older man—in his seventies JB guessed—and Jewish. JB got this because the old man looked exactly like Golda Mier, the Israeli leader, except he was balding and wore a pair of heavy black framed glasses. As JB came toward him he slipped the glasses off and set them down on the desk he had been working at. He was dressed rather formally in a pinstripe suit, but in shirtsleeves while he worked. His coat hung on a hook behind him. The tie was one of those wide silk affairs straight out of the fifties; it even sported a handpainted lily that was supposed to be white but had gone a soft tan from age. Black elastic suspenders rode his shoulders and down to his waist, causing his trousers to form a U at the front under his belly. The old man looked tired. Weary. Fagged out as in the original sense of the word. As if he had been through it all and was waiting for it too simply end. He leaned forward on the office door to get a closer look at JB. As he leaned out he pushed at the rolled sleeves of his starched dress shirt. He asked, "So, what I can do you?" in heavily accented English. He was Polish, or German. Slavic anyway. "I'm Ben," he finished.

JB stepped to the door and smiled, fully prepared to tell one of his more momentous lies if he needed too. He wanted to get inside John Weatherwax's apartment. There was something in that apartment that would answer his questions. He knew it. Or, at the very least, there was something in there to give him something to clarify it all some. If a lie would get him in then what the hell?

"I'm Jeremy Bent. I have a letter..."

That's when he looked at the old man's thin arms leaning on the door. White hairs grew sparsely and wildly on mottled pasty age spotted skin. Then JB noticed it. And he understood why the man seemed as he did. There was a faded tattoo on the back of the old man's right wrist. A two inch line of faded blue numbers that had forever marked his life. JB knew the numbers were from a long ago Nazi camp. This old man had survived in the truest sense of the word. JB could never know the depths of desperation this man had witnessed, but he did have a sense that they shared a common pain. Death was now scything his way through his gay community just as it had all those years before in the ghettos of Europe. There were even uninformed ignorant people today that suggested they should revive those camps to isolate the sick and afflicted of his kind. JB gulped, then went on.

"...a letter from the employer of one of your tenants. John Weatherwax. He's passed away and I've been sent to check on his pet." He held out the letter. Maybe the truth would work here, if the old man even cared. JB felt there wasn't much that the guy cared about anymore.

"What? He's dead?" He tsked. "Poor man." He looked down for a moment. Perhaps in remembrance? More likely it was pity at deaths ineffability? Or knowing of his own oncoming mortality? Then he looked back up. "Oy." A hand went to his cheek. "The rent? So, who'll pay? He owes?" He sat at the desk and opened a ledger. At a page he ran a finger down a line. His livelihood had quickly replaced any sympathy he might have felt.

JB spoke up. "I'm sure something can be arranged

with his employer about the rent. The address and phone numbers for him are there in the letter. As I said I'm only here about the animal. I don't want to take anything from the apartment. Have the police been by here yet?"

"What? No. No police." He sat back in his chair. "He's paid for the month. Good, yes?" He put his glasses back on, then leaned in again to read the letter.

"Then may I check on the dog?"

He waved a hand. "Yeah, yeah. I will call Harry. He'll take care of it." He looked over at JB. "This boss will pay the next month's rent you say?"

"He might. You should call him." The old man had picked up the phone on his desk and dialed. Then he cradled it again. "Harry will take you." And he bent to the letter again as JB heard the elevator running in the shaft behind him.

The doors opened and another man stepped out. He was looking at the small black box he held in his hand. His pager. He was maybe seven or eight years younger than Ben the manager. That made him fifty-eight or so. He was short and blocky in body type. An African-American, he had gray frosted hair cut close, and there was a jauntyness about him. As if he was content with his lot. He was dressed in a green twill shirt and pants with tan work boots. "Yeah, boss?" he said.

In a rush the old man explained to him who JB was and why he was there. He nodded, turned back, and introduced himself to JB as Harry, the maintenance man. JB suspected he was the person that really ran the building, with Ben being mostly an absentee owner. He stepped away from the office door and waved JB over to the elevator.

As he pressed the up button, he said, "Poor little dogs been crying all day for her owner. You gonna take her?"

"I'm going to check on it to make sure it's all right. I'll take it out and let it do its business, and feed it. That's all."

"Um-hum."

They stepped into the elevator car and Harry pressed the number six button. The car started rising. On the floor Harry led JB down a hall, turned a corner, and then stopped at a faux wood painted metal door. JB could hear the whine and scratching of a trapped animal behind it.

Harry searched a ring of keys attached by a chain to his pants, then used one of them to open the apartment. A tiny dog started yipping as he pushed on the door. JB looked down. What was the animal's name? Something silly wasn't it? Oh, yes, Sweets. Short for Sweetdarlingcutiepie.

Sweets was tiny—about the size of one of those butter cookie tins aunts send nephews for Christmas—and looked to be a compilation of breeds. A poodle and dachshund mix he'd been told. It could be. It certainly had the long body and short legs of the hund and the head and tail of a poodle. She was colored a reddish brown with fur that had the same look of his mother's old Persian Lamb coat. The hair was short and wavy. Caracal they call it. The dog's ears draped like her hund ancestors while her snout was definitely of poodle origin. A Poodhund? A Dachsoodle?

What JB couldn't fathom was the ugly part. Why did everyone he'd talked to think this engaging little dog was so ugly? The little animal was downright adorable. Really, really, cute. Teacup sized. Bright eyed. The shape of her nose even made her seem to be smiling. At that particular moment she was hunkered down protecting her turf. Bearing miniature teeth and yipping a little bark at the two intruders. But you didn't believe it for a second. The eyes betrayed her. They were huge and black and soft and loving. Since there was a dainty pink bow in the tuft on top of the head, JB said, "Ah, what's the matter little girl?" then stepped forward and bent down. Sweets instantly turned over and exposed her belly. A cream puff. JB reached forward and rubbed. Sweets licked his hand. "You must be hungry." He stood and checked the shelf over the counter on the right.

He found a can of food, searched for the opener in a drawer, and placed the contents on a plate. He set it down. Sweets gobbled at it hungrily.

"Looks like you've made a friend," Harry said.

"The last thing I need is a dog."

"Um-hum."

That's when there came a woman's voice calling Harry's name. It came closer, and then a gray haired lady in a bathrobe stuck her head into the apartment door. "Harry," she fluttered, "I have a leak in my sink faucet. I need you to fix it."

Harry rolled his eyes. "I'll be right back." He left the apartment following the woman. JB heard him say, "Okay, Mrs. Levine, let's have a look at it."

"Not look. Fix."

JB took in the small apartment. It was only a room really. Maybe twenty feet long and nine feet wide. On the right there was a combination oven and two burner stove that sat on top of a small refrigerator. A counter and shelves were built in next to it. A single bed with a satin duvet cover and a pile of pillows was farther along the same wall. Behind JB there was a separate bathroom with a claw foot tub, a toilet, and a pedestal sink. On the floor was a cat box that somehow Sweets had been trained to squat in. JB wouldn't have to walk her after all, but he would have to empty and change the litter before he left. A floor to ceiling window was on the back wall behind the end of the bed looking out onto Columbus Avenue, with the fire escape balcony outside it. With the noise from street traffic it must have been an adventure to sleep in here. A maroon velvet drape heavy with a muslin lining and matching fringe and tassels hung to one side, probably used to deaden that noise. Next to it was a desk with a shelf above it. The shelf was stuffed with books. An Italian Renaissance style curved chair sat in front of the desk. The left wall had a Grand Rapids bureau with a small TV set on top. Framed pictures hung along the wall and filled in the space to the door. A closet was situated between the front door and the bathroom. It was a long rectangle of a room that was a paragon of utility and economy. How much space did a man really need anyway? JB wondered what Weatherwax had paid each month for the place? It couldn't be much. Good location, low rent, a space saver single room. For New York it was terrific. For anyplace else it was a dump, as Bette Davis might opine.

Sweets finished with her meal, pawed at JB's leg, letting a whimper carry her wishes. He bent and picked her up automatically, not even thinking about it. He carried her on his arm and petted her as he perused the pictures Weatherwax had hung to decorate his tiny place. Again, for JB, it was an indicator of who a person might be. What kind of character he might have. It appeared Weatherwax was a naturalist. He had what looked like three really good California landscapes similarly framed and hung. JB moved to the bookshelf over the desk. Many art books. Van Gogh, Matisse — Ah, ha, and one on Chagall. He pulled that book from the shelf, laid it on the desk and opened it to flip through the pages. The illustrations looked exactly like the drawing he'd seen at Jathan's.

He put the book back and looked around the room again. Hadn't Bevan said that Weatherwax was an art collector? Then where was all the art? Other than the three landscapes and a framed pencil sketch over the bed, there were no paintings or drawings or art pieces in the room. JB supposed it was possible that they were in storage in California, but most collectors JB knew weren't willing to stash their collections in some storage facility. They wanted to see and touch the pieces they owned. To display them proudly. So where were this guy's things?

JB noticed a photo album sitting on the desk. He sat and opened it up. Photos could tell volumes about someone too. Bevan Jones had said that Weatherwax had only just moved here from Southern California, so JB expected to see pictures of beaches and palm trees. He found exactly that, with Weatherwax himself in the foreground of most of the photos. Weatherwax posing with his little dog held up to his face, smooching at her. Weatherwax being flamboyant in swim trunks. Sitting in a convertible. In several of the photos he had an arm draped over the shoulder of another man. One picture had Weatherwax and this other man with the dog scrunched between them. Was the man a friend? A lover perhaps? Not if the look on the man's face in the pictures had any say in the matter. Weatherwax's friend looked positively grim in almost all of the photos of him. Especially the ones that showed Weatherwax being the slightest bit affectionate toward him. His body language definitely was closed off to any of Weatherwax's overtures. What was most interesting was that on closer inspection the man with Weatherwax looked just like Jathan Holt. The hair was longer, and he was scruffier in the way he dressed and groomed himself, but it sure looked like the artist JB had met a few days before.

Okay, now that was very interesting. Was it possible Weatherwax and Jathan had known each other before he was hired to paint that bookstore window? The pictures in the album were definitely taken out on the West Coast. New York didn't have that kind of surf, sand, and sun combination. But Jathan lived here in New York. Maybe he had made periodic visits out West? Or did this man in the pictures once again raise the specter of some other person? One that looked exactly like Jathan. A twin then?

JB slipped one of the pictures out of the album and put it in his backpack, then began flipping through the album again. Photo after photo of the same two men. There had to be some sort of something going on there? At least on Weatherwax's part. There were more pictures of Weatherwax and the Jathan doppelganger. In a car. At a party. At the beach. There was something that had brought these two men together. The photos were solid evidence that Weatherwax thought it was a personal thing between them. It maybe wasn't so much for the Jathan lookalike.

Harry returned to the room. "Sorry I took so long. You find everything all right?"

JB quickly laid the album back on the desk. "What do you mean? I was just straightening up. Not snooping if that's what you're implying..."

"Um-hum. I was talking about the stuff for the dog. Her litter and all."

"Oh, no, I haven't changed it yet." He stood and realized that he still had Sweets in his arms. He'd been petting her, unconsciously, nonstop, while he'd looked at the album. He sat her down on the floor and headed for the bathroom to fix her box. Sweets was quick on his heels following after him.

A half full bag of litter was stored under the sink. JB bent to retrieve it and found Sweets with her paws up on his thigh, wagging her puff of a tail. "Not now, Sweets," and he pushed her down. JB emptied the plastic tray in the toilet and turned the water on in the tub to wash it out.

"Why don't you take the little dog with you?" Harry offered. "That way I don't get any more complaints from the tenants about her whining. You got everything you need right here. Won't even have to buy anything for her. Go ahead. It looks like she likes you." As if agreeing Sweets jumped on JB's leg and yipped at him.

JB put the cleaned box back in its place, then stood. "What the hell am I going to do with a dog?"

"Companionship?"

"Pain in the ass is more like it. You have to take care of animals. It's like having a perpetual toddler around all the time. I don't even have houseplants in my apartment for that very reason."

"Then maybe you need someone to liven your place up? Place must be like a morgue without even a plant to keep you company."

JB was stopped cold. Maybe Harry had accidentally hit on something. Maybe that was what he needed? Some livening up. He realized the man had a point. Without even knowing him Harry had hit on what was a damn good reason for the malaise that had set in on JB of late. Why he'd been having such trouble sleeping. With the AIDS epidemic ravaging and decimating his circle of friends he had been dealing with far too much loss. He realized that if it wasn't for Len there would be nobody at all. Perhaps it couldn't hurt to deal with a little bit of life for a change. And Sweets certainly was little. And affectionate. JB hadn't even known that he'd picked Sweets up again. The dog was happily licking at his cheek.

"All right. I don't like the idea of leaving her all by herself anyway. Is there a shopping bag around that I can use for her stuff?"

They found two Bloomingdales Brown Bags and loaded them with the items that Sweets would need. Her litter box, cans of food, the bag of litter, toys, and the soft bed she would need at night. A leash on her collar and JB was going down in the elevator with his new pet. "You'll pay for this, Harry. I'll get you, I swear."

All he said was "Um-hum."

※※※

JB was quickly out at the Avenue flagging a cab with the two shopping bags in his hands and the leash held in his teeth. Sweets was politely sitting beside him on the sidewalk. As he waved at a passing cab JB noticed Rex Reed go by him and turn the corner. Probably on his way to the Dakota. A half of one point at best.

Home was JB's first destination, then he planned to head down to Jathan's loft. He needed to have a talk with the man about what he'd found in John Weatherwax's apartment. The pictures had brought up several questions only Jathan could answer.

Chapter 13

HE COULDN'T DO IT. JB had planned on arriving home with the dog's stuff, then confining her to the kitchen area—so she wouldn't make a mess in the rest of the apartment— while he would go on to Jathan's place to have that talk he wanted to have with him. But when he put the dog down and started closing doors to trap her he caught a glimpse of the animals wondering little face and knew he couldn't just abandon her. Not again. The poor thing had to be feeling completely scattered right then anyway.

First, as far as the dog was concerned, her owner had left her adrift. That in itself would be a traumatizing event for anyone, or animal in this case. Now, she's been picked up and taken by this total stranger to be put down in another completely new and unknown environment, and then he's going to turn around and leave her again? It would be enough to freak out even the most hardy of souls, but this poor little dog? It just wouldn't be fair. He and Sweets had only begun to bond—the dog to him and vice versa—so leaving her alone now would certainly break whatever small amount of trust she might have in him. Forever. There was no other option; he would have to take her along with him.

"All right, Sweets. You get to go for a ride. Okay?" JB got the leash and snapped it onto her collar. It was a pink plastic confection with glittery rhinestones attached along its length. Sweets wagged her tail happily. He was really going to have to do something about the leash though. Expensive as it might be, nevertheless, it was much too California Queen for JB's taste. Something in studded black leather perhaps? Does Calvin Klein do dog accessories?

JB had to give major praise to Weatherwax. Sweets was beyond well trained. She was perfect on the cab trip down to Ninth Avenue, lying calmly in the seat next to JB, her head and paws resting on his thigh. There was a moment when they arrived and she resisted the leash, but it was simply for a call of nature. JB waited, Sweets finished and walked good as you please with JB to Jathan's loft.

✣✣✣

Starzy was bent down, reaching out to JB's little dog. "Oh, isn't she..." She hesitated a moment, searching for the right word. "Uh...sweet." She began to pet her. As for Sweets, she was loving the attention and wagged her tail like a metronome keeping time to a polka.

JB, was finally beginning to understand how and why Sweetdarlingcutiepie had received her nauseatingly saccharine name. Often when people don't want to insult someone they will use the kindest word they can come up with instead of saying what they really feel. Much the same as Southern women who say "Bless your heart." when they really mean "Back away bitch or I'll slice you like Mama Jean's Thanksgiving yam and marshmallow delight."

With this dog "sweet" was about as kind as most could come up with. Even JB had to admit that Sweets wasn't Westchester Dog Show material. "But she has the sweetest disposition I've ever seen. She's a total cupcake." JB picked her up and looked into her adoring eyes. "Doesn't her?" he cooed. Sweets licked his nose. He laughed, then set her back down on the floor.

Jathan led them all over to the living room area where he slouched down onto the couch, and raised his legs along its length. Sweets saw this as an opportunity and jumped up onto the cushions herself.

Meanwhile, Starzy played hostess and asked JB if he wanted to eat his dinner. "We saved you some Moo-Shu. I can heat it up. I don't cook but I microwave like a demon." She smiled. It was meant to forgive her anything and it usually worked.

"That would be great. Thanks." JB sat in the chair opposite Jathan. "Now Sweets, you get down from there. This isn't your home."

She had made herself snug in Jathan's lap, curling into a ball and closing her eyes for a quick nap.

"Friendly little thing isn't she?" Jathan began to stroke her back. "It's okay. Leave her be. So, did Len tell you my big news? Oh, by the way, thanks for getting me out of that mess with the police. I really appreciate it."

"Len said that you had got a one-man show out of all the publicity from this mornings event. I guess congratulations are in order, despite the unfortunate circumstances. Which gallery?"

"The Cochran over in Soho. It can make me..."

The Cochran was a newly opened gallery on the Soho art scene—it had been started the year before by the nephew of a more established gallery owner out of Chicago. It was located on the outskirts of the art district, but had drawn a lot of attention with its avant-garde exhibitions. It prided itself on featuring the newest of the new. Jathan's graffiti art would fit right in.

"Won't making your reputation depend on what the critics say, Jathan? Good luck with them. They can be very nasty. Especially with any work they don't understand. But, it does sound like a great boost for your career. And you certainly have more than enough paintings to show." JB indicated the rack stuffed with canvasses in the studio. As he looked back there he also noticed that the Chagall drawing was no longer sitting on the easel. Where had that gone, he wondered?

"Jathan, I'm going to be honest with you..." JB was finding out that sometimes this outright honesty thing could be the best way to go. Surprisingly, people tend to respond favorably to the straight forward unvarnished truth. Who woulda guessed? His putting it right out there had certainly got Jathan's attention. At least he'd stopped petting Sweets and was watching him. "Better yet," JB said, "As an explanation for what I'm about to ask, has Len told you about me? How I've solved a few crime cases in my time?"

"He did. Plus, I read one of your books. You snoop around where you're not welcome, stir things up, and end with solving the crime...pissing off the cops no end, right?"

"Ouch. You know that's almost hurtful." So much for favorably responding to the truth. So bluntly put it made JB out to be not much more than a buttinsky maiden aunt. Maybe Len's constant references to him as a Miss Marple clone weren't so far off the mark after all. "Okay, I get that it's the truth, but it still smarts. I'm not so sure I like being all this honest after all." At any rate he didn't think he'd become a fanatic about it. For now he'd just trudge onward. "Anyway, I've been looking into this Weatherwax killing. Especially after you became a suspect, Jathan. Trust me, I don't believe you did it, but there have been a few questions that have come up along the way, and only you can provide the answers. Do you mind if I ask?"

"That's the snoopy part, right?"

"I suppose. I'd rather think of it as solving the puzzle. The answers to my questions simply fill in the blanks. Like the *Times* crossword puzzle on Sundays. It's only the writer in me. Plots need to be complete in and of themselves. Readers hate it when you leave big gapping holes."

"All right," he said. However, Jathan seemed wary, not at all sure where JB was going with this. "Go ahead. You can ask. But I don't guarantee the answers will be what you what to hear."

"I'll take my chances. Okay. First, how well did you know John Weatherwax?"

Jathan physically relaxed. His face softened, he dropped his shoulders, and he took a small breath. It must be an easy question to answer for him. "Not very well," he said. "Only from our few meetings at the bookstore."

"Then you hadn't known him anytime previous to his calling you to do the window painting job? From before, maybe? Out in California?"

"Was he from California? I didn't know that. Nope, only at the store. Why?" He was wary again.

JB pulled the photo from John Weatherwax's album out of his backpack and held it out toward Jathan. "Then tell me who it is that John Weatherwax has his arm around in this picture?"

Jathan looked down at the picture. His head dropped so he wasn't looking at JB anymore. His jaw went slack and he simply stalled, much like an automobile on a cold morning. He was unable to respond for a very long moment. He did sit upright on the couch, putting his legs flat to the floor, which caused Sweets to move off his lap.

JB filled in the silence with his own answer. "You do have a twin, don't you, Jathan? Another person who looks exactly like you is somewhere out there." JB made a sweeping gesture toward the outside. "He's the one who killed John Weatherwax. Not you. That's it, isn't it? Why haven't you told the police about this man?"

Jathan stared at the picture while he spoke. His voice was flat, like soda pop left out to long. "I hadn't seen him for years and years. His name is Robin. Mine's Jay. Mother's name was Dovie. She had a thing for birds. That's Robin in that picture." He grabbed it away from JB. "And, yes, he's my twin. We got separated when we were put into foster care. We were six. We lost touch. I didn't even know he was still alive until a few weeks ago. And I didn't know he knew John Weatherwax. I swear."

Jathan still sat on the couch, staring at JB as he crumpled the photo in his hand, making a fist around it. JB wasn't sure if he was going to attack or was keeping himself in check with the gesture. They continued to stare at each other, neither one willing to make a move.

Starzy set a plate of hot food in front of JB and held out both a fork and a set of wooden chopsticks. When JB didn't take either of them she set them down softly on the table, as if any clatter they might make would disturb the silence between the two men. Would be the cause of some destructive upheaval that might start and never stop. The actress in her had tumbled to the dramatic moment.

She went around the table to sit next to Jathan on the couch, which made Sweets have to move further down. She circled a couple of times and lay down again. Starzy took Jathan's hand into hers, pried open his fist, and took the creased photo from it. She laid it on the table and smoothed it out, taking it in. Her head swung back and forth between the two men, still on their Hispanic stand-off. Then she shifted and looked straight into Jathan's eyes. "You never said anything about a brother, Jay Nathan. Not ever."

Jathan pulled his eyes from JB and took Starzy's

hand. He spoke directly to her, as if JB wasn't in the room. "In foster care I found out real fast it was better to not ask about him. Nobody ever would do anything to help me find him. In fact, I got beaten when I did ask, so finally I just calmed up and didn't ask anymore. And then I didn't think about him much. I was more interested in surviving. Robin disappeared from my life."

Starzy took him in her arms and held him close. "Oh, you poor dear boy. To have to grow up with that hidden away inside you. You could have told us, Jay Nathan. Mom and Pop would have helped you. We might have found your brother..."

This was getting away from where JB wanted to go with this conversation. He interrupted them.

"Then you hadn't seen him? Until a few weeks ago you said? What happened then?"

Still facing Starzy, he said. "He showed up. Here. One morning he buzzed the apartment and suddenly, bang, I had a brother again. It was so weird. This person who looked exactly like me was standing across from me, talking like there was some sort of relationship between us. I didn't even know him. Who the hell was he? You know what I mean?"

Starzy nodded vigorously. "I think I do, honey. It must have been quite a shock." She took him in her arms again.

"There is something else I wanted to ask you about, Jathan." JB wasn't going to let this go. He needed his answers and he was going to get them. "When I was here in your loft last time there was a drawing on that easel over there. It's gone now. What happened to it?" JB was well aware his question might seem off the mark when Jathan had just made such a momentous confession, but he suspected the two things were tied together in some fashion and this was the clearest path to getting it all out.

"You're asking about the Chagall drawing, right? I gave it to Robin."

And there it was. JB had his connection.

"But it wasn't a real Chagall drawing was it? It was a copy you'd done yourself. Was that what your brother wanted from you? I mean, for him to show up out of the blue like that. There had to be something he wanted from you. He wanted you to forge a Chagall for him, right?"

Jathan nodded, then he added. "But it wasn't a forgery, JB. It was a copy. I only did a copy for him. I'd done it before. Lot's back when I was a student. It was no big deal. I did a Miro copy for him first, then the Chagall. But I didn't put on the signatures. So there wasn't anything illegal about it...even I know enough of the law to know that the signature is what makes it a fake. Plus, I cheated. I signed it with my initials."

"You did? Where?"

"Like I always do. I hid them in the picture. You just have to look for them. They're there. I didn't think it would hurt. Robin told me it was a replacement for a friend who loved Chagall's work. It was a gift for him. To replace a couple of damaged works. He said his friend's other drawings had been wrecked in their move."

"I would hazard a guess that the friend was John Weatherwax. Once they had the drawing it would have been easy enough for them to add a fake signature to it. After that was done they were able to perpetrate their forgery scam on some unsuspecting mark." JB had a sudden flash. "And I think I know who the mark might be."

Chapter 14

USING JATHAN'S PHONE, JB punched in the private number Bevan Jones had written on the back of his business card. He checked his watch. It was a little after six PM.

He didn't think Jones would mind JB taking him away from whatever business he might still be conducting at such a late hour. Workaholics often used interruptions by others as an excuse to stop working for the day, especially when they couldn't admit that they wanted to stop anyway. Then they wouldn't have to blame themselves for what they perceived as slacking. When Bevan answered he did seem pleased when JB said hello.

"I was hoping I'd hear from you..." Bevan's voice was underlined with a Pyrrhic triumph. JB had picked up a phone and called him instead of it being the other way around. Type A personalities, like Bevan, put a great deal of stock in such idiotic signs. These alpha types always needed to stay on top. JB thought it was merely tedious. "You want to have that dinner we talked about?" he crowed. You could hear the exultant smile pasted all over his tone.

JB responded, "It's early for dinner. How about drinks. I could meet you..."

"No, that won't work. I'm going to be busy for the next hour or so..."

JB figured either he really was busy or it was simply a ploy on Bevan's part to maintain his control over the situation. Ho hum, does it really matter? To Bevan it probably did. To JB it was, so early in whatever games Bevan was playing with him, only mildly amusing and it would remain amusing only until JB got the information he was looking for.

"Where are you?" Bevan went on. "I'll come find you."

Which would put JB in a waiting pattern, standing around at Bevan's beck and call. Good God, didn't the man realize top or bottom only meant something in Cole Porter songs and during sex — and even then it was usually better to be a little versatile. JB stifled an urge to grind his teeth, then gave him Jathan's address.

"Hey, that's just around the corner from where I am. Why don't you come here in say...twenty minutes? We can go for drinks from here." Control, control. The man would seem to be an unrepentant power freak. Bevan gave him the address he was at and they hung up.

If that conversation was any indication of the

way Bevan Jones was going to conduct himself on this "date" of theirs, then JB could guarantee he wouldn't be spending any great lengths of time with the man. JB decided that if Bevan made even one reference to himself in the third person he would be waving a long good-bye to the man. This sort of jockeying was exhausting and ridiculous, and JB just didn't have the patience for it.

Starzy gathered up her things so she could leave with him, while JB said his own good-bye to Jathan. He wanted to make sure Jathan would be available if what he believed about the Chagall drawing should pan out. Jathan would be needed then to verify his suspicions. Starzy got into her coat and kissed Jathan on the cheek. JB snapped the leash on Sweets.

Carrying the dog, JB and Starzy went down to the cobbled brick street below. They walked the block over to the Avenue together, then said their own good-byes when Starzy flagged herself a cab. JB waved as she disappeared uptown, then turned and began to walk the few blocks over to the converted warehouse that Bevan had given him directions to.

The meatpacking district JB was walking through was fine during daylight hours but after the work day it got deserted very quickly. Stores were shuttered, safety grills were pulled down, and the people who worked in the area would quickly abandon the area.

Then it was pretty much deserted, at least until the late night dance clubs geared up. With the sun setting the streets JB was walking through started to become shadowy. And ominous. He quickly went past dark waste can and dumpster filled alleys rife with blackened deeply recessed doorways. Slacked electrical lines crisscrossed overhead, along with hanging rusted metal fire escapes. They cast heavy shadows over everything — a screeching cat followed up by the sound of a falling tin in one of the alleys gave him reason to feel still more anxious. It got worse each time he passed another one of the perfect mugger hideout spots. Damn his overactive imagination. He needed to get a grip is what he needed to do.

He knew Sweets wasn't going to be much help. Her tiny teeth wouldn't do damage to a Twinkie much less a two hundred pound mugger. Although her frantic yipping might be enough to chase some attacking ninja rats away.

The warehouses around where JB had been sent were all closed by the time he arrived. The one he had been directed to look for appeared to be abandoned, as did the entire block it sat on. Built of battered unwashed yellow bricks, it piled up to a three story building, with crowned mullioned windows along the upper floors giving thin indications of any life going on inside. A couple of dim lights shining from floor two were the only hint of any activity inside.

Steel pull down doors lined up along the road side of the building. Tattered flyers pasted on them crackled in the breeze created by the cars speeding past on the adjacent highway. JB had to walk all the way around the building, past flat brick walls with tall weeds climbing up them, past loading docks with their raised wooden walkways and tangled wild undergrowth below.

Finally he found a doorway with a buzzer and a speaker box. Beside the door, under a single industrial shaded light, was a sign announcing inside was the company called *Wild Bull Productions.* Bevan's production company. The company logo featured a humanoid cartoon bovine dressed as a construction worker wearing a flannel shirt, denims, and work boots. And it was winking. A cross between the Greek Minotaur and a character from the Village People.

JB pressed the buzzer and waited.

A tinny spectral voice issued from the box asking who he was. Once satisfied he was expected it buzzed open the door.

JB stepped inside to a dusty concrete hallway as a voice down at the other end said, "This way." He headed in that direction, picking up Sweets to hold in his arms. Like the dog would act as some sort of shield? She'd hide by sticking her head in JB's armpit is what she'd do. Which was exactly what she did do. The dog was no dummy.

At the end of the hall JB found a pudgy youth with bad skin, a dirty T-shirt, and a clipboard clutched to his chest.

"Follow me," he said in a squeaky disinterested voice. "Mr. Jones is waiting upstairs."

He turned quickly and disappeared down the hall. JB started after him. They both stopped at an open elevator shaft and waited there while the boy pressed a brass plated button. Soon enough the old-fashioned open platform freight elevator slid into view. The boy pushed up the wooden gate when it stopped and they stepped on. Then he pulled on a piece of hanging rope to bring down the gate. He pressed the button for the second floor. The mechanical whirring of years old gears ground and screeched as the platform wheezed its way slowly upward. JB had absolutely no idea what the hell he was going to find when the second floor finally came into view. A group waiting to yell "Happy Birthday"? A madman with a chainsaw to chop them into pieces? A bacchanalian orgy?

That last one turned out to be the closest.

As the sign at the door had stated the floor held a working film company. Or, to be more precise, a pornographic video movie making enterprise then in the process of taping a naked gay sex scene between two very hot looking men.

The boy with the clip board held up a hand to halt them, saying "Wait until they call cut..." JB looked out on the vast open floor to an isolated pool of light against the far wall. Several heavy duty lights on stands surrounded the ersatz set. At the center was a gym setup consisting of a barbell bench and a rack of weights against the raw brick wall of the building. Lying on the bench was a nude young man who at that moment was being screwed royally by another equally nude young man.

Over to the side, in the dark area, was a picnic table that was holding various pieces of film equipment. Sitting at it was the director watching a hooded TV screen that was showing the action being taped by a cameraman on set with a professional video camera. Going direct to tape the director didn't need to worry about sound —the grunts, sighs, and "fuck me harder's" would all be looped in later—so he was shouting instructions to the men being filmed as if it was in the days of silent movie making. "Raise your leg, Barry, you're causing a shadow. Pull out slower Dirk. We want to see that big cock of yours. Zoom in for the close-up, Paul."

Standing behind the director was Bevan Jones, his head swiveling between the TV screen and the actual action. The director finally called, "Cut," and the set physically relaxed.

Towels were thrown to the two actors as the video operator stood and stretched his legs. Another man came in from the darkened sidelines and started adjusting the lights. There was an audible rise in the amount of noise as the crew of about ten went about their various jobs. The director left the table and walked over to his actors.

Bevan turned to look at JB, smiled, and waved him forward. When JB was next to him he snorted, "What's with the little dog?" He pointed at Sweets cradled on JB's arm. "Don't tell me you're one of those God-awful poodle queens? That'll play hell with your butch image."

JB pulled his eyes away from the actors still on the set. One of them hadn't covered himself with his towel and was sitting on the weight bench for all to see. His cock was hanging a lengthy tumescent eight or so inches from a neatly shaved and trimmed crotch, the towel hanging nonchalantly around his neck, showing a total lack of concern at his nudity. JB did so love an exhibitionist. This one with a full hard-on could have been a human sundial.

"My image is fine, thank you. And it certainly doesn't need outdated clichés like that to define it. Not that it matters, but this dog belonged to John Weatherwax. Your employee, if you remember. I'm taking care of him until you find his heirs. If he had any."

Bevan held up his hands. "Hey, I didn't mean to piss you off. I was only teasing."

"Sorry. It's been a long day. I'm holding her because I didn't want the dog to run onto your set barking and ruining your shot. This is quite a setup you have here." JB hoped he hadn't ruined his barely budding rapport with Bevan. Even if he did see him as a total jerkwad he didn't want to completely alienate him right off. "Do you do all your filming in studio?" Get him talking about business. That's always a safe topic with these types.

"Mostly. We can make this place look about anyway we want. Office, gym, store, motel room. It's easier than going somewhere outside on location, and way cheaper. Got to keep the bottom line down you know."

"With the kind of profits you told me porn makes these days? I bet you could film at Tiffany's and still be under budget."

"This is more cost effective because I own this building. My apartment is on the next floor up."

"The whole floor?"

"Yep."

How handy, JB was thinking, the man has a built in sexual marketplace on one floor and a playground on the other — with bed and room service provided. Hugh Hefner was the only other person JB could think of that had it so good, but then he was only in it for the articles...

"Is that where you keep your art collection? Upstairs? I'd love to see it."

A change of subject it may have been, but JB had to get Bevan going where he needed to go to get what he wanted out of him. But then Bevan, once again proving JB's sleaze hypothesis of his character, turned what he'd said sexual.

"That can be arranged," he said with what he thought was sexually charged innuendo. "I'll take you up there in a little while, cute stuff." He reached out and touched a finger to JB's cheek followed by a wink.

Oh, crap, how was JB going to manage this? He was about as interested in having sex with Bevan as he was in congress with one of the aforementioned Mr. Hefner's bunnies. JB really was *only* interested in the articles.

The video director had returned and was sitting at the table again. Bevan turned back; his interest in JB put on hold while he watched the taping. Type A's would always turn to business before any other kind of pleasure. Even sex. JB then was just supposed to wait, completely ignored and forgotten in the background.

"Okay, let's go for the money shot," the director ordered. "Dirk, are you ready?"

JB smiled, and said outloud. "His name is Dirk? Really? If I was going to pick a porn name it would be something way better. Maybe something more to the point. Like Frankie Friction...or Chubby Poundacock?"

He got no reaction. Total silence from the two men in front of him. They were far more interested in what was going on out on the set.

Dirk, the exhibitionist, was flipping his cock on his hand working it hard, while his partner arranged himself on the workout bench. Once lying on his back he lifted his legs in the air, and waited.

"Where's the fluffer?" Dirk called. "I need wood here."

The director yelled, "Fluffer!" and the boy with the clip board appeared in the light. He went to his knees in front of Dirk, took that huge dick in his hand, and proceeded to suckle him until Dirk had risen to his full girth. Dirk pulled away, turned, moved into his partners open legs and entered him. All very business like. This was, after all, his job, and time was money.

Dirk began pumping. A couple of minutes later he pulled out, ripped off his condom, and jerked his cock to ejaculation. A huge wad of white jizz slammed out and landed on his partner's chin. Then his ass pushed another onto the man's chest, and with less velocity, another wad splashed on his partner's stomach. The director called, "Cut."

Dirk grabbed a towel from clipboard boy to wipe at himself.

"That's why they call em' money shots, baby. That'll add a good twenty or thirty to the gross." Bevan slapped the director on the back, congratulating him. "And you got it all? You did, didn't you?"

"From two angles, boss."

JB, awed, said, "How'd he do that? There was so much cum."

The director answered. "No sex for two weeks before the shoot and massive doses of Vitamin E everyday the week before. Impressive, huh?"

"I'll say."

"It also doesn't hurt that he's only twenty."

"I'll say."

※※※

Bevan took another swipe at Sweets on the short elevator ride up to his apartment. "I have a question," he said. "If a gay man's girlfriend is a fag hag, is his canine bitch a fog hog?" He snorted at his joke.

JB didn't look at him, but simply petted Sweets. "Nope," he replied. "The bitch would have to be the one asking the question." He smiled. And waited for a reaction...

Bevan roared, his laugh going on while the car came to a stop and he raised the gate. "I like you, Bent, you've got balls."

"Only the regulation two. And unlike those men downstairs mine aren't all primped and trimmed and shaved. What's with that anyway? It's like an unattractive house, you know, a little shrubbery helps with the curb appeal." JB bent and tied Sweets to a chair leg by the elevator. Then he stood and looked out on the apartment.

It was a nightmare of modern minimalist decor gone overboard. The flooring was a smoothly poured concrete with colored pebbled patterns embedded in stream like curves and waves. There were occasional islands of leather and chrome foam slab furniture sets, thick glass tables on silvered bases, white faux-fur rugs, arching silver ball floor lamps. All of it in a football field sized loft. Areas—bar, entertainment center, a pool table, even a hot tub—were divided by hanging curtains of silver chains. The right wall was a row of paned industrial windows covered with floor to ceiling polished wood panels that swiveled to let in light. A long wide hallway on the left was his art gallery. It was lit by a rack of hanging spots on dimmers that ran the entire length of the loft. Other rooms—kitchen, bath, and bedrooms—were through doorways interspersed with the art on that side. Expensive it certainly was. Tasteless and pedestrian it also was. It was as if Bevan had decorated by lifting entire pages from the latest issue of *Metropolitan Home* magazine. It had all the warmth of a hamster cage.

"So this is where you live? It's exactly what I would have expected." Before Bevan could respond JB went on. "That's your art collection in there, isn't it?"

JB aimed over to the hallway and began to look at the paintings hung along the walls. They might not exactly be up to MoMA standards, but they weren't all that bad either. Along with what pieces JB had seen hanging in Bevan's office the collection itself bordered on very good. There was a signed Picasso, several good abstracts by a couple of mid-level abstractionists, and a Warhol screen print of Elvis. And then JB spotted the familiar Chagall drawing dwarfed by sitting in an oversized rococo gold frame.

"Is that the drawing you bought from John Weatherwax?" JB asked. "The one you said was stolen?"

"Yeah, that's it. I got it back this afternoon."

"So you paid the ransom?"

"I wanted my drawing back..."

"I hope it wasn't a lot..."

"It could be considered substantial by some, but for an original Chagall it was minimal."

And there it was. The opening JB needed to drop his atomic art bomb. He plunged ahead.

"Are you sure it's an original?"

"What? Of course it is. I had it authenticated by experts at the Metropolitan. They vouched for it."

"Before or after the robbery?"

Bevan was looking quite flummoxed. "It was before," he said slowly. Now he was becoming worried. "Why?"

There was no easy way to give it to him. "Because that's a fake, Bevan."

So, JB just put it out there. Bluntly. Straight forward. How was Bevan going to take the news was the next question?

In only the turn of a minute JB felt almost sorry for the guy. Bevan's face went white as he took in what JB was saying.

"According to a knowledgeable friend, you were a player in a very old con game."

Bevan's jaw dropped, and then he shook his head. "No. No. He ran a hand through his hair. "I had it checked out. It's real..." He backed away and went to a couch to sit.

JB followed him. "John Weatherwax made you a real good deal on the drawing, didn't he? Almost too good to be true, it was so cheap..."

"Because his mother needed some fast cash."

"There's always some reason for needing immediate money. Then he even handed over the drawing so you could verify its originality." Bevan agreed. "Once that was done you happily paid him and sent off your bargain to be framed. Weatherwax knew that, didn't he? Which frame shop you sent it to?" Bevan waved a hand for him to go on. "Weatherwax then had it stolen from the frame shop by an accomplice and they hit you up for a ransom. Does this sound right so far?" Bevan moaned and nodded again. "So, you paid the ransom, and got the drawing back. Everyone was happy. But, what you got back...that drawing hanging in there...is a fake." He pointed to the hallway. "That Chagall drawing was done by an artist I know just last week. Weatherwax and his accomplice stung you. You were taken."

"I don't believe you. How can you be sure?"

"Do you have a loupe? I think I can prove it to you."

Bevan stood and went over to a glass topped desk where he searched in a wire basket. He came back with a small photographer's loupe. While he was doing that JB had gone to the hallway and took the drawing down from the wall. He carried it back to the couch and set the frame on the coffee table in front of him. He bent over it.

"Do you mind if I remove this from its frame?"

Bevan acquiesced. JB flipped the frame over, removed the paper backing, pried up the staples that held it in, and took out the drawing. And with that action he spied his first clue that he indeed had the fake. There were tiny brown spots dried along the bottom of the piece. It wasn't foxing; it was the stains from Len's spilled *Snapple*.

It only took another moment and JB was looking through the loupe at the drawing. He scanned it looking for the name he knew was hidden somewhere in it. Jathan had said he'd put his initials in it.

He found them in the violin playing bunny's tail. Amongst the curves of the fluffy appendage were the two initials. A J and a H. They clearly identified the drawing as a fake. He held the loupe out to Bevan.

"There." While Bevan looked JB said, "Do you see them? They stand for Jathan Holt. That's the artist I mentioned. We can take it to his studio if you want. It's pretty close. He'll be glad to identify the drawing as his own."

Bevan sat up straight. He spoke, but mostly to himself. "But it was so beautiful...and at such a good price." He set the loupe down beside the drawing. "Yes. Let's do that. I want to meet this artist. Those could just be a smudge of the lines done by Chagall himself. It might only be a smudge..."

It was clear Bevan didn't want to believe that he'd been taken. No victim of a sting ever does. How much had he lost on this fake Chagall? "Substantial" he'd said. That could mean anything. But JB was pretty sure it was in the multiple thousands. How many he didn't need to know. And he would bet that Bevan wasn't going to say anyway.

To paraphrase a classic movie line it hadn't been beauty that took down the beast; it was arrogance and greed. Every scam that has ever been run by every con man since Carlo Ponzi has begun with the same two elements, and Bevan had them both in abundance.

Chapter 15

BEVAN STOOD UP from where he was sitting and returned to the desk. He began to look through the wire baskets he used to hold his office supplies.

"What are you doing?," JB asked.

"I don't appreciate that I've been jacked around this way. Any more than I was happy paying a ransom to a pack of thieves for my own drawing. I took precautions."

He took out a typed sheet of paper from a file folder he'd pulled. "I have a list of the serial numbers on every bill I gave those bastards. Now, I'm going to follow up on it."

JB could see the underlying anger present in what Bevan's was saying. He wasn't going to stand for some twenty-five cent con man getting his hands on any one of his dollars. Not without putting up a fight anyway. He picked up the phone and punched in three numbers. When there was an answer he directed the person on the other end of the line to come up right away. He turned back to face JB.

"My head of security. He'll have some ideas on how we can clear this up."

"What's to clear up? You paid the money. The con men have probably skipped town already."

"The ransom was paid less than three hours ago. They couldn't have gotten very far in that amount of time."

There was a chime at the front of the loft as the door slid open. A man stepped in and walked across to where JB and Bevan were standing.

✻✻✻

Now this is much more like it, JB was thinking on seeing Bevan's security man. This is way more to my taste.

The security man was a raging beauty at about six foot three inches tall. He was built like ex-military. That background was also obvious in the way he carried himself. He had the ramrod posture soldiers will affect. And what was always a turn-on for JB, he was a redhead. His short cropped hair was a light ginger tending toward a salmon blond. He also had the pale translucent lightly freckled skin that went with the hair—that was a yum—with piercing opalescent eyes—a yum doubled—and he had a jawline that could open a tincan. As pretty a man as JB could ever hope for he could serve as one of Nathan's models in any of his homoerotic pictures. He was dressed in pressed black jeans and a tight fitting yellow T-shirt. JB wondered how he had got the soft cotton material of the shirt to hold military uniform creases? Then again they could simply be a part of that body. The man didn't salute Bevan, but JB wouldn't have been surprised if he'd stood at attention in front of him. "Yes, sir," he snapped. His hands went to his back, crossed, and rested.

"When you delivered the ransom was the money as we discussed, Rex?"

So the guy's name was Rex, huh...Rexes? King? Head Honcho? Commander? Mr. Big? Sir? Again, Sir. Please, Sir...JB shook his head, his imagination was running wild.

"As you requested we put an electronic tracker on the envelope, sir. We'll know where the money is very soon. My men are coordinating the address now. We should have it located momentarily."

JB asked. "So you were the one who picked up the drawing?"

Rex looked first to Bevan, who nodded, then pivoted to face JB. Almost as if he was giving a book review in grammar school he reported, "We handed the cash in its envelope over to a hired bicycle messenger. He then handed us a plain brown paper wrapped package with the drawing inside. We had the messenger followed, of course, but soon lost him in the afternoon traffic. It's a bitch to keep up with those guys. They zig and zag through the cars so fast they disappear. As I said, we had a tracker in with the cash so we've been tracing the address for it since. We've got it narrowed down to the Upper West Side so far..."

"The Upper West Side, huh? I think I might be able to help you with that address..." JB explained where Weatherwax had lived and his own supposition that the accomplice might be using the same apartment for a hide-out.

"Get the drawing, Rex, we have some traveling to do." Bevan got his coat and started for the door. Rex picked up the drawing, and followed after him. Rex it would seem was very much a lapdog type of fellow, always following after his master. Although he may have a few ideas of his own he was excellent at carrying out other peoples wishes. Subservient. Submissive. Yum...

"Hey, wait up." JB shouted. He went over to the door and picked up Sweets, who'd been sleeping where she'd been left. He grabbed his own coat and went to where Bevan and Rex waited in the elevator.

※※※

They rode down to the second floor. Rex stepped off and went directly to his own office, leaving the two men waiting.

Once there he slipped the drawing into a cardboard portfolio and then into a tote bag with handles for easier transport. He put on a military shoulder holster with its pistol clipped in, and slipped on his own black leather coat over that. Armed, he was prepared to go. A robot ready to attend his masters needs. To certain segments of the gay population this guy was a shining jewel. A diamond for the rough.

Bevan rubbed at his chin. "I think I want to stop at this artists place first. I need to know for sure if that drawing isn't real. JB, you said he would identify it..."

"As his own work, Bevan. His place is only a few blocks over. We could walk it."

They started the elevator going downward again.

"No need for that. I have my car."

※※※

The three men left Bevan's warehouse and once on the street Rex broke off to go get the car. JB turned to Bevan

"It's really not that far, and the dog could use the walk. Why not just give Rex the address and you and I can hoof it?"

Bevan checked his watch. "I suppose you're right. It might be more direct."

"Faster in the long run," JB agreed.

It was one of the great disadvantages of having a car in New York City—warrens of one way streets butting up against each other along with impossible parking conditions.

The black luxury sedan pulled up beside them.

Bevan bent to the window and spoke to Rex, then turned back to JB. "Okay, let's go." The two of them began to walk toward Hudson Street.

Even counting the time it took for Sweets to do her business JB and Bevan still beat Rex to Jathan's loft. They went to the door and buzzed. No answer. JB buzzed again. Still no answer. He backed out to the street and looked up at the window. It was dark inside.

"That's odd. I wonder where he's gone?"

Rex pulled up behind the men and stopped, letting the car idle.

JB shrugged. "Well, it doesn't matter I guess. We can do this another time can't we? Why don't we go on to the apartment? The longer we futz around here the more time the grifter's have to get away."

Bevan agreed and reached for the car door, pulled it open, and indicated for JB to get in. JB gave Rex the exact address of the building and sat back. The car spun its tires as it accelerated toward the West Side.

✳ ✳ ✳

Rex let Bevan and JB out in front of the apartment building just off Columbus Avenue, then drove off, with Sweets lying peacefully in the back seat, to find a parking place.

"Should we wait?" Bevan asked.

"It could take a while. This neighborhood is always crowded."

The apartment entrance, now smoky gray in the faded light, still had the original white glass and silver metal light box hung over the door. With both linear and curvilinear deco lines it proclaimed the building as the *Torkey Apts.* in a blocky font not seen since the Thirties. The door into the lobby shone a rectangle of yellow out onto the concrete of the sidewalk. .

JB bent to look inside, then stood. "What are they doing in there?" He headed for the door and yanked it open.

"What?" Bevan started after him.

"Come on. Jathan and Starzy are in there."

JB went inside, with Bevan behind him saying, "Who?"

"What are you two doing here?" JB asked, sounding almost offended by their unexpected presence in the lobby.

Starzy turned with startled wide eyes at his abrupt question. "Oh, dear. Hello JB. I-I came here to meet Jay Nathan. He called." She weakly pointed to him standing next to her.

"It's my fault. I asked her to meet me. I got a call from my brother. He's here. I wanted to confront him about that drawing. But I didn't want to do it alone." He put an arm around the girl's shoulder. "So, I called Starzy to help me."

"Your brother? Your twin brother? He called you?"

"That's right. He said he was leaving town tonight. After I'd only met him a couple of times. And there was that drawing thing. I wanted to see him before he disappeared again."

"So that's why you weren't at the loft. We stopped by to have you check something for us." JB then introduced Bevan to them. He shook Jathan's hand.

Bevan got right to the point "This is the artist that did the fake Chagall then? I'm glad to meet you. I have the drawing with me. I was wondering if you could identify it? We'll need that identification before we can prosecute anyone."

Jathan smiled. "Of course. I'm so sorry that my work has been used like this. I didn't mean for it to be."

"So you really weren't aware it was being used to run a scam?" JB asked.

"No, not at all. Robin only said it was to replace a print for a friend of his. I had no idea they meant to use it to steal from anyone."

"Robin?"

"My brother. He's upstairs. I'm supposed to meet him."

That's when Rex came into the lobby from the outside. He had the tote bag with the drawing in it tucked under his arm. Bevan quickly had him take the portfolio out, open it, and hold it out for Jathan's inspection.

He took a moment to run his eyes over it, then identified it as his work. "But I didn't put the signature on it. That's not my doing. It must have been added after I gave it to Robin."

"And that's what makes it a forgery," JB added. "At least in the eyes of the law."

Bevan handed the portfolio back to Rex. "I want to meet this guy. This con artist. Of course, what I really want to do is to beat the holy crap out of the guy, but the police wouldn't look too kindly on that I suppose. Rex, you have your weapon?"

Rex reached into his coat and nodded.

JB held up a hand. "So, you're going to shoot him?"

"Of course not, although he deserves it. Instead, I intend to take this Robin person into our custody. He's a wanted man, isn't he? We'll make a citizens arrest. Then we can hand him over to the cops. They'll want to talk to him."

"What do you intend to charge him with? Aggravated hoodwinkery." JB pushed the button for the elevator. "Actually, what the cops will want to charge him with is first degree murder for the death of John Weatherwax."

The five of them crammed themselves into the small elevator and rode uncomfortably, shoulder to shoulder, up to the sixth floor. The door slid open and Rex more or less fell backward out of it, which made it easier for the others to step into the hallway. JB led them to the hall leading to Weatherwax's apartment door.

They stopped. Crisscrossed as an X on the doorway were two strips of yellow police tape, with an official looking flyer taped to the door warning that it was a crime scene. The cops had obviously been there since

JB's last visit.

Starzy said in a whisper, "Do you think he's in there? Did he cross the police line?"

Bevan sighed. "He's a criminal. I don't think police tape means a hell of a lot to him. Go ahead, knock," he said to Jathan.

JB watched as he timidly moved to the door. Rex pulled the pistol from his coat and aimed it.

Jathan softly rapped on the door. Then he stepped back, in case, like some Warner Brothers gangster movie villain, Robin should come bursting out of the apartment with a machine gun blasting and growling "You won't get me coppers."

There was no answer. An anticlimax at best.

Jathan turned back to the rest of them. "He said he'd be there."

"Maybe he went downstairs to the deli for coffee and bagels?"

Bevan didn't seem to appreciate JB's suggestion. He snorted then said, "Rex, break it down?"

"Its metal, sir, I'd break my shoulder before that door gave way."

"Has anyone tried the knob?" JB stepped forward and turned it. The door opened a smidge. He pushed on it so it swung open fully.

It was dark inside. JB reached around the jam and flipped the light switch. "He's not...Oh, shit. Yes he is."

JB pushed the tape aside and took a step inside, with Rex stepping into the doorway directly behind him.

On the floor, with a large pool of blood spread out to circle like a halo around his head, was a dead man. Since he was lying on his stomach, there was no way to know exactly who it was, but from the build of the victim JB had a good idea. He took another step in. At the doorway all of them crowded up, looking over Rex's shoulders to see what JB had found.

Starzy, her hand to her mouth, asked, "Who is it, JB? Is it..."

He bent down to look into the face of the dead man.

It was Jathan. Or rather it was Robin, Jathan's twin, since Jathan was standing in the doorway looking in, his face gone pale, his eyes wide with shock.

Chapter 16

"HIS THROAT'S BEEN cut. Sliced like a pound of deli ham." JB was bent down looking at the wound on the man's neck. "Ear to ear. In one continuous cut. Very neat. Almost professional. There doesn't appear to be any signs of a struggle. I'd say he was probably attacked from behind."

"Everybody stay in the doorway." Rex was doing his ex-MP thing by taking over and issuing orders. He took one step into the room and stood still, being careful not to disturb anything. "There's not enough room in here for all of us. Let Mr. Bent and I check out what there is to see."

"Its fairly obvious," JB commented. "The dead man was planning on taking off and someone...an undetermined someone at this point...objected to his plan."

JB then stood and looked around, copying what Rex was doing. Neither of them moved about but looked with squinted knowing eyes at the various tells left in the room by the assailant.

There was an open suitcase on the bed, partially packed, which would indicate the victim was getting ready to leave for places unknown.

Next to the suitcase lay an art folder, which JB, using a pen he pulled from his pocket, flipped open. Inside was yet another Chagall drawing. Whether this one was a fake or the genuine article, JB couldn't be sure without closer inspection.

JB noticed the dead man had fallen forward, landing face down on the floor. This was an indicator that he'd been attacked from behind, and made it clear that the person who killed him was someone the victim knew. He'd let his killer into the room and then turned his back on him.

Rex spied an eight by ten manila envelope on the desk, which he recognized as the one he'd delivered the ransom money to the bike messenger in. It was now empty. The money was gone. Taken by the killer probably.

There was no murder weapon evident anywhere in the room. But it was clearly a thin knife or blade that had sliced open the victim's neck. A switchblade, as the killer had used on Weatherwax? Or a straight razor? Or an artist's *Exacto* knife. Or something from the kitchen area? Whatever it was, the killer seemed to have taken it with him when he left.

JB remembered that the door was open when he had come into the apartment. The killer hadn't taken the time to find the keys and lock it as he left. Maybe because he knew that Jathan was coming to the apartment momentarily? So the murder timeline had it happening within the past hour or so. That was also clear from the blood spill around the victim's head. It was still a liquid, barely sticky. It hadn't begun to coagulate yet.

JB knew the dead man was the killer of John Weatherwax. The police had a video that showed him committing the act. He also knew the murdered man was Robin Holt, Jathan Holt's twin brother. The police didn't have that information yet. It had to be Robin. And Robin's killer was? Well, it could be anyone couldn't it? Robin might have had another accomplice involved with him in his scam? Maybe that's what he and Weatherwax were arguing about before Robin stabbed him in the window of the bookstore? Had there been another person Robin had taken up with? Was John Weatherwax jealous? An element of jealously had been the motive for countless murders. Was that what was at work here?

※ ※ ※

Rex, his arms crossed over his chest, had it all figured out.

"Here's how I see it," he said with an unequivocal certainty to his tone. "The dead man here..." he used his toe to indicate the body on the floor. "...was packing up and leaving. Another person, unknown to us, got into an argument with him...probably over the ransom money paid for the drawing...and it escalated. The unsub then caused this man's death using a sharp instrument to slit his throat. Possibly a knife. Or some other kind of blade. Once he was dead the killer took the money and skipped out leaving us to find the body."

Well, JB couldn't fault him on his conclusions, but it was all a bit redundant at this point. JB had that all figured out already. It looked like Rex was going to take the part of Inspector Lastrade to JB's Sherlock Holmes. Not quite as astute as Watson but still good to have around if only to prove JB's expertise.

"Then you're assuming there was a third person involved in the scam with Weatherwax and this guy."

Jathan said from the doorway, "His name was Robin. He was my brother."

"I know this must be shocking for you, Jathan. But remember you didn't really know him, did you? You said he'd only just contacted you a few weeks ago."

"That's true, but it's so weird. Seeing him lying there. Looking the same as me. It like seeing myself as a corpse. So strange." He turned from the doorway and scrunched down in the hall, his hand scrubbing at his eyes. Starzy kneeled beside him to comfort him.

But JB had another question for Jathan, regardless of any distress he felt over his brother's death. JB picked up the drawing from the bed and carried it out to the hallway. He bent down next to Jathan and held it out. "Can you tell me if this is another fake? Or might it be the original?"

Jathan took the paper and examined it, then handed it back to JB. "I think that's the real deal. The signature looks real enough. It's not my work, I do know that."

JB took it back to the room. "That's how the scam worked." He held up the drawing. "This was the real Chagall that they would use as bait for their designated fish. To sucker the mark into the sting." He handed the drawing over to Bevan, who was standing in the doorway. "That drawing is the one you originally sent to the museum to be authenticated. Once that was accomplished they would steal it. In your case from the framers you'd sent it to. And then after the ransom had been paid, replace it with the fake. After that they could do it all again with someone else."

"Well, this is mine now. I paid for it. Plenty. It's my drawing." Bevan took the fake from its folder and handed it to JB, replacing it in his folder with the real Chagall drawing. "Put that piece of shit where the real one was. Let the cops figure it out."

Rex stepped forward. "That may be the best idea I've heard so far tonight. The cops do need to figure this all out for themselves. I'd suggest you go back home, sir. I'll stay here and call the police to report the murder. The rest of you should get out of here too. There's no reason to get any of you involved in this."

JB agreed, then added, "The police forensic team will probably get more bits and pieces that they can shove under their microscopes, but we've got all the clues we can from here. How are you going to explain to them why you were here?"

Rex shrugged. "I'd traced this art thief to this address. When I got here I found this guy lying here dead. None of the others have been in the room so none of them have left any fingerprints. None of them came in and disturbed anything. The cops will have to take my word for what happened. And that means that none of you were ever here. Except for you, Mr. Bent."

"And, I was here much earlier, as the super can testify to, so there would be a reason for my prints being in the room. All right, I suppose our leaving is for the best. And it's doubtful the cops will look any further. They'll get to close a murder case they have open on their books. They'll have John Weatherwax's killer. And he's dead. All tied up in a bow and finished. Case closed. They'll be happy with that."

JB stepped around Rex and went out to the hall. He went over and explained to Starzy and Jathan what they were going to do. "...to be honest it will serve no earthly purpose for either of you to get involved in this. The publicity wouldn't help your career, Starzy. Nor you're emerging art career, Jathan. So both of you should just go home. It was Bevan's security man that cracked the case, you guys weren't even here, right?"

"That's right," Bevan, who was now standing behind JB, agreed. "As a matter of fact I was in the editing room at my loft all night. I've even got several witnesses that will say so."

"And I was out walking my dog. Let me get Sweets and do exactly that, Bevan. She's still in your car."

"So, we're supposed to act like none of this even happened?" Jathan asked.

"Not so much that it didn't happen...more like all of us were somewhere else when that man was murdered. Which is really the truth. You simply need to pretend you haven't been here tonight."

Chapter 17

AND THAT'S EXACTLY what each of them did.

He wasn't sure about the others, but for those first few days JB would jump every time the phone rang, sure it was the cops calling about some piece of evidence they had found placing him at the scene. The doorbell ringing would give him heart palpitations. Then after a week without any calls or visits from any members of the constabulary his paranoia cooled down and he was able to get back to doing his own work.

Sweets had settled in, happily taking over and running the household like it was her own personal fiefdom. JB was at her beck and call for walks, food, and general petting when necessary.

Starzy hadn't given up trying to get JB to sell her the screen rights to his novel. She had decided to stay on in New York, keeping after him, constantly nudging at him to relinquish his work to her. She was also becoming a visible part of the New York social scene. Written up almost daily in the *New York Post* as being out and about, here and there—at *Elaines* for dinner, at *The Russian Tea Room* for lunch, in negotiations with Hal Prince for the next Sondheim musical. It was the usual PR BS for actresses who were not currently working.

Often seen with Starzy on these publicity soirées was Jathan — he was using just the one name now, giving up his last name, like Madonna or Cher or Mussolini. He was relentlessly out to advertise his upcoming one man art show. Every artist, in one way or another, soon realizes he's only a fur covered fedora and a gold tooth away from being a whore with the media. JB had his book tours. Len was always available for talk shows and interviews. Starzy did fashion layouts for newsstand magazines. It was all the same.

But Jathan had managed to put his own spin on getting known. Aggressively so. He'd engineered a couple of very public brouhaha's that the gossip columns gobbled up. One night at *Elaines* he'd told Norman Mailer that he was a hack. Mailer punched him. Then another night, at a disco, he told reporters that Andy Warhol was an artistic sell out. Andy would have just shrugged.

Jathan was quickly becoming the latest bad boy on the New York art scene. All of it not much more than posturing from JB's point of view. Jathan was trying to place himself as a new style gay man. He wasn't swishy, or nellie, or any of the other clichés often attached to homosexuals on TV shows and in the movies. No carrying purses or owning pink poodles for him. He was a bad dude only skirting the edges of gayness. A homogenized aggressively masculine—read more acceptable for the great unwashed public—gay for the press to discuss. He was a gay you could take home to mother—if mother was Alexis Carrington from *Dynasty*.

※※※

It was two weeks later and Len, sitting on JB's couch of an afternoon, was regaling JB with the latest from his ACT-UP meetings. "So, there was this big argument going on about whether or not to have a protest, and finally Larry Kramer...I told you about him, didn't I, JB?"

"Yep. he's the firebrand that started the group, right? He also wrote *The Normal Heart*, and started GMHC, before they asked him to leave. I know who he is."

"He is a piece of work, our Larry. Well, like I was saying, he never pulls his punches, so he stood up in front of the whole group and shouted, 'Damn it. We have to escalate the noise we make so we'll be heard...' Well, the whole room stood and applauded. It was something. It's no more Mister Nice Gay, JB. We're standing up for ourselves."

"It's about time. I've always wondered why we let the breeders get away with what they do to us. At the last pride parade I was thinking that if all those people that were marching didn't go to work the next day we could bring the whole country to a screeching halt. Can't you picture it? Nancy Reagan screaming through the halls of the White House for a hairdresser. Any hairdresser."

"Stand Up. Act Up. Fight Back. Fight AIDS. That's what we say at the end of the meetings. It's so true, JB."

"I hope it works. Something's got to be done. You know, I have a funeral *and* a memorial next week, Len. That's three services this last month alone. Its not right."

"Your preaching to the choir, brother. Or is that

sister? Is there soda in the ice box?"

He got up and went toward the kitchen. Sweets was right at his heel, following after him. She had somehow intuited that Len wasn't crazy about her, and she wasn't going to settle for it. She liked him. He should like her.

"What is with this animal, JB?" Len, soda in hand, sat back down on the couch. Sweets jumped into his lap, tail wagging, making herself comfortable.

"She wants you to like her, Len. Dogs can sense when you're bigoted toward them."

Len picked her up and moved her, setting her down beside him. "It's not only her. It's all dogs in general. You know when you hate only one dog its bigotry. When you hate all dogs its consistency. I'm simply not a dog affectionado."

Sweets climbed back onto Len's lap, still wagging her tail. Len, not thinking, automatically started to pet her, then realized what he was doing and raised both hands. "And this one...I swear if I had a dog this ugly I'd shave its butt and teach it to walk backwards."

"Len, that's downright mean. Come here, Sweets." JB clapped his hands. She jumped down from Len's lap and ran to JB. "Her isn't ugly, is her? Her is sweet as candy." He picked her up and rubbed noses. Sweets licked his nose back.

"Egad. And him is really sickening. Capital S. Capital ick. Capital ning." He sipped his soda. "So, there's going to be this ACT-UP action at the pharmaceutical company Saturday after next."

"Next Saturday? That's the same day Jathan's art show opens. How are you going to manage that?"

"What's to manage? Are you listening? The protest is the week after, besides, I am a working actor, JB. On Saturday's I have both a matinee and an evening performance. Remember? I will have to miss both events. Not that Jathan would care."

"What? There's trouble?"

"We've decided not to see each other anymore."

"You both decided? That doesn't sound like you."

"Okay. He doesn't want to see me anymore."
"He dumped you? I don't believe it."
"I'll get over it, okay."
"Of course you will. It doesn't take much more than a shower for you to get over any of your affairs. But you're usually the dumper not the dumpee."

Len tried for blasé. "Not this time. He hasn't returned any of my calls. So it's over. Like that." He snapped a finger.

"He has been acting up lately. And not in any sense you were talking about before. Even Starzy said something about it the other day."

"Its fame, JB. You know what it can do to some people. A little publicity can go right to one's head, like champagne bubbles or a good Scotch. It's the hangovers that'll kill you. He's going to have a doozy of a fall if the critics turn out to hate his work. He'll hit bottom real fast. You know how you torture a gay man, don't you? Throw him into a bottomless pit."

"Oh, you are so bad, Len, but I suppose you are right about Jathan. He seemed like such a nice boy though."

"You're still talking with Starzy are you?"

"Oh, sure, she still wants to get her hands on the rights to my novel. Her lawyers...the firm of Flushour, Furphy, & Furry, if you can believe it."

"It sounds like a firm of bunnies."

"Hare appellants..."

Len groaned.

"Anyway our lawyers got together last week and hammered out a contact. But I haven't signed it yet."

"Why? Isn't the money any good?"

"Not bad. Substantial without being overly flashy. And it's only for a six month option. If they don't get a workable script that I approve of it reverts back to me. But the problem is what you brought up the other day. I wonder what they'll do to my book. Will they destroy its integrity?"

"JB, its Hollywood. They don't even know that the word integrity exists. Take the money and run. That's my advice."

And that's exactly what JB did.

On the next Saturday he met Starzy for an early dinner before the two of them would go on to Jathan's art show opening. He explained to her he would sign the option if it would stipulate that JB had nothing at all to do with the script. He wouldn't be consulted. He wouldn't take credit. Not even a mention that it was adapted from his novel in the film's credits. He did want a first reading, but that was it. He would then make any suggestions he felt pertinent, and those they could take or ignore. It was their choice. Starzy was ecstatic. She had got what she wanted—through blatant manipulation and a bit of chicanery maybe—but she had it. She admitted that she had already started a writer working on a script. He had promised a completed first draft in less than a week.

✳✳✳

The art gallery where Jathan's show was being held was a beacon of light on the dark street in Soho the building sat on. The hanging canvas flags announcing the gallery and Jathan's show flapped in a slight breeze that moved the stale night air. Steam rising from sewer vents lay soft to the ground and gave the scene a surreal Daliesque feel entirely appropriate for an art gallery opening. A scene out of *Mummenshanz* was being enacted inside as crowds of fancy dressed people milled around the lighted interior. When JB opened the gallery door for Starzy sound from inside wafted out, assaulting their senses and creating a muted sense of excitement as they entered.

It was your typical gallery opening. Mediocre white wine served in plastic cups, cater waiters carrying soggy appetizers on silvered plastic trays. People more interested in being seen than seeing the art crowded in islands about the gallery. Exuberant hellos and air kisses abounded. A few of the patrons would wander from painting to painting making pretentious noises as they passed. There was a stir when a couple of B-list celebrities came in. Abe Vigota, who used to play a character on *Barney Miller*, the now defunct sitcom, came first, then a few steps behind him, Pia Zadora, who was more famous for her name than any real talent, made an entrance on the arm of some second ranked European tennis player.

JB and Starzy got a ration of wine and a paper napkin holding some gelatinous pink substance smeared on a wheat cracker and started working their way from picture to picture. They stopped in front of a small canvas called *The Pickup*. It was a shoulders up portrait of two men on a darkened street, a match lighting a cigarette highlighting the comely face of one of the men.

"Do you like it?" asked a voice behind them. They turned and recognized Bevan Jones. "I just bought it." A thin young women with too much eye make-up under harlequin framed glasses stepped up and put a red dot sticker on the description tag beside the painting, indicating it was sold. She smiled at Bevan and moved on. "It's a bit more illustrative than I usually like but it spoke to me."

"Reminds you of a past experience does it?"

He grinned. "Got the T-shirt."

"Me too. It's the reason I still carry matches when I stopped smoking two years ago."

Bevan laughed, then asked, "So how have things been?"

It was an innocuous question shaded with an undertone that made it clear he was really asking about that night a week before.

JB answered lightly. "Nothing to report so far. All's quiet on my end."

Starzy nodded. "Mine too."

"So, what went down with Rex?" JB lowered his voice. "I'm dying to know what happened when the cops arrived at the apartment."

Bevan shrugged, continuing his own nonchalant pose. "Ask him yourself. He's out by the car." Bevan took Starzy's arm and led her away, which left JB to make his way out to the street.

Bevan's car was parked a couple of spaces down from the gallery entrance. Rex was leaning against the front fender eyeing the people passing him. He was dressed in a dark Italian cut suit that outlined his body, a dark shirt with matching tie, and sunglasses — even if it was night time. He was as JB remembered. Poster boy gorgeous, if not the sharpest knife in the drawer. Now how the hell was he going to ask him out?

As JB went toward him Rex reached into his coat pocket and pulled out a pack of cigarettes, tapped it on his hand, and put one to his lip. In a gesture echoing the painting he'd seen inside JB lit a match. "Let me get that." He held out the flame. Rex leaned forward, cupping the match with his hands.

"Hi there," JB said. "I came out to ask you what happened when the police arrived at the apartment last week? How did they react to the body?" There was no preamble to the question needed. They both knew what they were talking about.

Rex raised his head and exhaled a plume of smoke. "It was all pretty business like. Another dead guy was no big deal for them. I told them my story. The detective in charge wrote it down, and that was it. They let me go."

"And there's been nothing else?"

"I got a call a few days later from another detective at another precinct. A Lieutenant Greenberg. He wanted a statement."

"That's the same cop I spoke with before. About John Weatherwax."

"Then it was the police closing that case. It was all pretty routine. The detective did mention that the dead man's brother...that would be Jathan, right?" JB nodded. "Well, he'd identified the body and had a funeral home pick it up for cremation. And that was it. Not a word since."

"Then maybe we skated by on this?"

"That's what I think. As long as we keep our mouths shut we shouldn't have a problem."

Ah-ha, there it was. An opening. JB knew what

he had in mind was extra cheesy but it could work. Go ahead. Throw it out there.

"Alright, but I warn you. I know tongue-fu."

"What?"

"I can beat you into submission with my tongue." He raised an eyebrow.

Rex reached up and lowered his sunglasses. Oh-oh, maybe it was more of a throw-up line?

"Is that a proposition?" So, he wasn't so dull after all. He'd got JB's innuendo at least.

"Only if you want it to be."

"I could be interested."

"Then maybe we should discuss safe words..."

❊❊❊

JB returned to the gallery, a phone number in his pocket, just as Liz Smith with her entourage arrived. She gave the art a cursory walk around, and left immediately on her way to some other event happening that same night. JB went looking for Starzy and found her talking with the gay newspaper columnist Michael Musto. No surprise that he was there since he'd admitted openly that he would attend the opening of a paper bag if invited. Starzy was busy simply doing her job. Schmoosing. One should never pass up a chance for a mention in anyone's column. JB stepped up and made his own bid for notice.

The gallery owner, a butterfly of a man with squinty eyes and pomaded hair, was happily glad-handing his way from group to group. And making excuses for the fact that Jathan himself wasn't there yet. He was informing everyone that Jathan had been told to arrive a half hour after they started. "But he's being bad," he would chuckle. It was now going on an hour and a half after the opening and he still hadn't arrived.

The art work that was hung on the walls did surprise JB a bit, erotica always being in the eye of the beholder. Male nudes didn't bother him. Male nudes' being tortured and bloodied just wasn't his particular cup. The prices being asked were the most surprising, considering this was a first show for the artist. They were asking several thousands for even the smallest paintings, much more for anything larger. And Jathan was showing his older pieces, all dated during the last couple of years. One was even done almost ten years before. The show then was more of a retrospective pulled from that rack of paintings in his loft than any of his more recent art. But there were red dots on the tags next to several of the pieces. They had sold. That always created good buzz for any artist. When the art critic for *ARTnews* came in and seemed approving that got a rise from the crowd too. More red dots soon appeared.

It was at that point that Jathan arrived. That single event ended up causing an almost riot. Both doors of the gallery slammed open, rattling them on their hinges. Every person inside turned to look. Every eye in the place focused on the door to see what the noise was.

In the wide open doorway stood a wavering and grinning Jathan.

To put it bluntly, he looked a mess—disheveled, unshaven, probably unbathed, and certainly on something. Booze, cocaine, some other drug, or a combination of them all wasn't clear, but he was sloppy and barely able to stay standing upright. He had his arms slung over the shoulders of two women, who would, in the next day's newspapers, be facetiously described as cheap. One particularly vicious columnist even going all the way to "slutty and skanky".

One of the women had bleached out teased straw for hair. She had on a few days old make-up, smeared lipstick and overpainted cheeks. The other woman was an African-American with an orange wig, giant hooped plastic and rhinestone earrings, and ample cleavage not being held in by a sequined tube top. In fact, both were dressed in what could only be described as hooker duds.

Mummers of shock rose from the gallery guests. The gallery owner, fluttering with anxiety, ran up to Jathan and tried to stop him from coming further inside. Jathan wasn't having it. He pushed the owner aside and raising a hand to the staring crowd, shouted, "What's up, bitches!" followed by a giggle worthy of the Joker of Batman fame. Then he staggered in, stumbling on the small step at the entrance. "Who put that there?" he said as he spun around and kicked at the step.

A wide hole opened as the gallery crowd backed away from this drunken apparition invading the gallery. Jathan let go of his escorts and spun again, grinning and laughing. "Whatta ya think, guys?" he trumpeted. "Great huh? Fuckin' artist, man. I'm a fuckin' artist..." He started to laugh again. As the laughter got louder it went more out of control. He was roaring, holding his stomach at the seeming absurdity of it all. He was staggering around the galley pointing at the works. And at the people which caused him more hilarity.

At that point the owner again tried to get Jathan under control by taking hold of his arm. Jathan pulled away, staggered backward, and banged against the wall. The owner went up to him again. "Come on, Jathan..." he pleaded. "...let's get you to the back."

"Hey, man, back off..." Jathan pushed at him with both hands. The owner stepped back then went in again, trying to save this awful situation. As the owner grabbed onto Jathan's sleeve he yelled at the poor man. "I said get the fuck away from me!"

Jathan grabbed the owner at his shoulder, then roughly pulled him close into his chest. Faster than a second and with more strength than it would have been suspected he had, Jathan slung his other arm between the owners legs, grabbed his thigh, and lifted, raising him over his head. Roaring some animal like unintelligible sound, Jathan then threw him, as a basketball to its hoop, at the front window of the gallery.

The owner flew, crashed, and shattered the pane of plate glass, landing outside in a shard covered heap on the sidewalk. People inside gasped and cringed, moving back and away from the violence Jathan had wrecked upon the gallery.

Jathan stood, now silent, wavering where he had

been, breathing heavily. Then he weaved over to the door, and like the monster in Mary Shelly's horror tale, waved his arm at the crowd behind him. He staggered down the outside steps and disappeared into the dark. The two women he'd brought with him ran up to the door, one of them turned and squeaked, "G'nite folks," wiggled her fingers at them, and followed after him.

JB turned to Starzy. "You can't tell me that isn't a man in chaos in search of frenzy…"

Chapter 18

THE ART GALLERY incident was reported on every media outlet the next day. TV covered it. Radio shouted it between playings of *Faith* and *Bad*. Every New York paper, including the *Times*, carried some version of the debacle. With pictures. Even Liz Smith, who wasn't even there when it happened, gave an "eyewitness" account.

Jathan had become, overnight, not only famous

but legendary. And, more amazingly, every story ended up praising Jathan's work. Against all expectations the art critics that counted were hailing him as the decade's most innovative new artist.

That was where the *Times* talked about Jathan's opening. In their Sunday Arts section. They used the story as part of their art criticism column. After reporting, with ever so much decorum, the incident from the gallery it went on to call his paintings *"stellar psychosexual explorations of the outsider milieu."* and *"virile explorations of alternative eroticism."* The art works *"combined classic illustration with cutting edge aesthetic abstraction."* Then it went on to call Jathan a *"latter day antisocial loner, following in the path worn by the likes of Jackson Pollock and Ernest Hemmingway before him."* It looked like being the bad boy had only added to Jathan's chaché.

The gallery owner wasn't hurt badly, a few minor cuts from the glass, a sprained wrist, and a very bruised ego. Jathan was, naturally, fired from the gallery — which gave him even more publicity. The gallery itself shut down with no re-opening date announced. The owner retreated back to Chicago to lick his wounds.

Every person who was there—and many who weren't—had a story to dine out on for weeks to come. Even the two hookers Jathan brought were interviewed and enjoying their own fifteen minutes of fame. And Jathan's art was suddenly very desirable and collectible. That is if you could find a piece to buy. Without a gallery to show them Jathan's paintings had become like hen's teeth, and were going up in value by the day.

❄︎❄︎❄︎

Len, having finished his Sunday matinee performance, was sitting in JB's kitchen reading that morning's *Times*.

"This must have been quite an interesting exhibition." He was reading about Jathan's opening, of course. "Aren't you glad you were a witness?"

"It was a miracle someone didn't get hurt. He was definitely out of control," JB said.

"Been there way to often," Len mumbled, as he went back to reading.

JB carried a cup of coffee over to the table and set it in front of Len. "But you were never destructive, my friend. This was way beyond anything you ever got up to. It was almost something psychotic. Incredibly disturbing anyway."

Len set the paper down. "It's all the same impulse, JB. Jathan intended to hurt somebody. Some thing. Mostly himself in the long run. We should go see him. I could talk with him."

"Would it help?"

"It's what the AA program is based on. It's one of the main steps. Helping others to see what a destructive path they're walking down. It's what I'm supposed to do when I see someone in this kind of pain."

"Well, if you think it will help." JB went to the kitchen door and took Sweets leash from the knob. She was at his feet instantly, wagging her tail happily. Walkies. Yea. He bent to put the leash on her collar.

"What are you doing?" Len asked.

"I'm taking her along. She can use some time outside. She's been cooped up in here since yesterday."

"Don't you think it a bit too precious? You and that little dog?"

"What are you talking about?" JB went to get his coat from the hook by the door. "Come on, Sweets," he called. Her toenails could be heard running across the kitchen tile toward the door.

"Its just too, too, gay, JB. Queenly in the extreme. A gay man with a tiny dog on a pink plastic leash?" He held out an arm and dropped his wrist. "Wooo," he shrilled.

"Oh, please. Let's face it, Len, the gayest thing about me is you. As you've just proven conclusively with that gesture." He stuck his wrist in the loop of Sweets leash. "Now come on, let go if we're going."

※ ※ ※

Jathan buzzed them into the building. Len started

up the ventilated metal stairs, with JB behind. Sweets pulled at her leash. Her short legs and small size made the stairs an obstacle greater than she could manage. "Opps, sorry, cute stuff." JB bent and picked her up, rubbed her head, then started up the stairs after Len.

At the third floor Len found that Jathan had left the sliding door ajar an inch or two. He rapped, then slid it open enough for him to enter. JB got to the floor, put Sweets down, and followed Len inside.

Jathan was lying on the couch, in the same clothes he had been wearing the night before. All he'd added was a damp cloth over his eyes, his obvious hangover seeming to incapacitate him. He reached up and removed the cloth. "You've come to see if I'm dead haven't you? I'm not, but, my dear God, I wish I was."

"You play, you pay," Len said, not allowing him much sympathy for his condition. When Len had been drinking he had been where Jathan was more times than *I Love Lucy* repeats. He knew full well that sympathy wasn't what was needed here. Why should he enable another person in their own excesses?

He sat in the chair facing the couch intending to give Jathan a straight as string talk about the results of this kind of behavior on his career and his life. A clear warning at this juncture, early in the progression of his disease, might be the very thing needed to save him. If Len had only known—then again, if Len had to be honest with himself, he probably would have still followed the same path he did. A drunk is a drunk and can only do what drunks do. Drink until they've had enough. Or die. Well, maybe Jathan would be the one who was different. Len leaned in.

As JB got close to the couch Jathan was lying on Sweets stopped cold, refusing to move, pulling the leash taut on JB's arm. He gave a tug, but Sweets stayed right where she was. He looked back and saw that the little animal was standing on stiffened legs, muscles quivering, bearing her teeth at someone or something. A growl rumbled deep in her throat. Then she barked. Only one to start. But that was prelude to more following fast upon it, one on top of the other as her yelping increased. It quickly gained in volume and feeling—anger and frustration and instinct mingling into a tirade of enormous proportion. Sweets was, for some reason, protecting, or protesting, or going nuts—JB wasn't sure which.

"What's wrong, girl?" JB said, stepping back to her. She continued barking, the sound piercing the air with its passion and resolve.

"My God, will you stop that damned yapping..." Jathan moaned and turned over, pulling a pillow over his face.

"I'll take her out to the hall. I'm so sorry, Jathan. I have no idea what's got into her. She's never like this."

An aversion to drunks and their aromas was JB's guess. Couldn't blame her. JB remembered Len had been pretty ripe quite a few times back in the day. The odor of old sweat, enhanced by the dissipating alcohol wafting from a man's pores could be off-putting at best. Or maybe it was the remnants of the day old puke clinging to Jathan's clothes. JB hadn't noticed it himself but since an animal's sense of smell was way more acute than any human it could be more disturbing for her. Sweets, however, looked to be protesting far too much, as Shakespeare would have it.

JB picked her up and while she squirmed in his arms, carried her out to the hall. He wrapped her leash around a convenient water pipe and told her to quiet down, wagging a finger at her. She cringed at his tone and lay down, quiet at last. He went back into the apartment.

※ ※ ※

Len must have said something that wasn't what Jathan wanted to hear because he'd sat up and was giving Len the proverbial unfeathered bird. "What the fuck!" he spat.

JB slipped into his chair and kept quiet.

"Is that a question or a philosophy?" Len asked bluntly. "Because your actions last night could easily make it either one. Don't you realize how bad crap like that can be to your career?"

"Are you kidding? The papers love it. They compared me to Pollock and Hemmingway for Christ's sake...."

"To a shotgun suicide and a drunk who died in an accident between a tree and his Ford. This isn't to be proud of, son? I'll wager you don't have a gallery to represent you today, do you? How much is that going to cost you?"

"You lose. Sure, I got fired, but I also got a call from the Margo Greene Gallery this morning. They want to represent me with my own show as soon as I'm ready. And I'll still get my cut from what pieces sold last night. And that was just about every painting I'd hung. So, fuck you. And that's a full out statement, not some stupid ethical question."

JB was figuring it out. Twenty or so paintings at the prices he'd seen last night would give Jathan a very healthy payday. Even if he was only entitled to a percentage of the whole. And the Greene Gallery he'd mentioned was far more prestigious than the one that had let him go. It looked like the lions wanted to eat at the carcass of the newest kill. At least until all the meat was gone.

"Jathan," Len pitched his voice to be as conciliatory as he could be, "You have to know that right this moment you're the flavor of the month. So you'll get away with shit like this for now. But if you keep this up, destroying relationships with the people who control the galleries, you'll eventually be thrown out with yesterday's rubbish. They simply won't put up with this sort of crap. Take it from someone who knows. There are too many people waiting behind you who want it more and won't give them these sorts of problems. I'm sorry if that's blunt, but it's a fact. The fine arts business is the just the same as my show business. Do you have any idea how lucky I am to have any career at all? I'm an openly gay actor in a straight controlled business. But, I work in the theater, and it's what saves me. If I was out in Hollywood I'd never get any work at all. Show business...or any other business for that matter certainly won't put up with a drunken gay actor. Or a drunken fuck up of an artist for that matter. Isn't that right, JB?"

"He's telling the truth, Jathan. It's exactly the same in the publishing game."

Jathan grunted, giving in an inch. "All right. I'll grant you that. Maybe you're right." He sighed, his shoulders falling. He looked from Len to JB with a sad, sorrowful, expression on his face. "But come on, guys, can't you cut me a little slack?"

He stood and went over to the shelves against the wall. He picked up a plain twelve by twelve inch cardboard box, came back to the couch, and placed it on the table in front of Len.

"That's my brother, Len. That's all I have left. A damned box of dirt. Don't I get a chance to grieve? To be sorry my one and only blood relative in the whole world is gone. Forever. Before I even had a chance to know him. Give me a break...please." He seemed as if he might be close to tears, his face screwing up to keep from actually crying.

Damn, JB was thinking, watching Jathan closely, this guy is good. You have to give him that. When Len was drinking JB had seen about every excuse known to man acted out by a pro. Every rationale, every invention Len could come up with for his bad behavior was rolled out and tried. JB had even fallen for a few of them. But this? This had to be the ultimate in manipulation. Using your dead brother's ashes?

"...I know what I did was wrong, Len." Jathan seemed to be on a roll. "It was all me. I'm completely to blame. I was so intimidated by the gallery atmosphere. I'd wanted that show for so long and there it was. My life's work out there. Open to the eyes of the world. To the critics. It was more than I could handle, that's all. It won't happen again. I'm so sorry..."

And there it was. The old "I'm sorry" ploy used by every miscreant from three year olds with a hand in the cookie jar, to bank robbers, to spousal abusers, to murderers. It is a song sung so often it has lost all meaning in the wallowing of its users.

"What are you sorry for, Jathan?" Len asked. "Are you sorry for making an ass of yourself last night? Or for being a sloppy falling down drunk? Or that I'm making you face what you've did?"

JB knew that next was the "It'll never happen again" part of the evenings entertainment. And it was true. It wouldn't happen again, JB and Len both knew that it wouldn't happen until the next time. Was Len going to fall for this? JB knew he knew better? AA had taught him something, hadn't it?

Len smiled a sad smile and reached out to touch Jathan's knee. His head swung back and forth in a tiny arc, then he looked Jathan in the eyes and said, "You know, all the reasons you just gave me here...those may be the most exploitive list of crapola I've ever heard. You really shouldn't try to shit a shitter."

JB stared at him. Oh, that's good, Len, add a little kerosene to the fire you've already started? Well, at the least Jathan's lament hadn't taken him in.

Len went on. "Just think about what I've said, kiddo. I've been here before, you know. I lost it all and have had to rebuild it all again. Actually, that's still a work in progress. It's a day at a time, and its not so easy this second time around, believe you me."

Jathan didn't respond, but instead sat staring daggers at Len. His anger had become his refuge from Len's outright exposure of his misbehavior. Len, finished with his efforts at reclamation, sat back and, gratefully, didn't add more fuel to the conversational bombs he'd already dropped.

There followed an elongated and uncomfortable silence as the two men sat across from each other. JB was stuck waiting for one or the other to say something. The next thing. Anything. He couldn't stand it. He decided to fill the sink hole that had opened up between them himself.

"When are you planning to have your next show,

Jathan?"

Jathan turned to face JB. "In a week or two. I can't afford to wait very long. The public forgets so fast. I may as well have the explosion before the dynamite fizzles, as they say."

Len snorted. "Who says? You know, considering your current condition I don't think you should be operating any metaphors right now. That was just wrong,"

Jathan ignored him and stood. "Do you want coffee? I want coffee." He headed for the kitchen to pour a cup from the pot in the machine.

JB also stood, relieved that the impasse had been breached. They could again talk like people instead of opposing forces. He headed back to the studio area and stopped at the work table. He turned to face Jathan. "With only two weeks you won't be showing any new work then. Right?"

Jathan came over, carrying his coffee cup, and stood on the other side of the table, facing JB. "Right. There won't be time. I'll have to use what I already have." He indicated the storage bins of paintings against the wall.

JB noticed a coffee can on the table with brushes sitting in it. According to the slight odor there had been turpentine in it once upon a week or so before. Any liquid in it had by now completely evaporated. He picked up one of the brushes and ran it against his hand. "But you haven't been painting for a while have you? This is bone dry." He hadn't meant it to sound so much like an accusation, but realized after it was said it did. Len had got out of his own chair by then and had joined them at the work table.

Jathan took a sip from his cup. "No, not really. It's been really exhausting the last few weeks. I've never stopped. Running everywhere. What with Starzy being here and us going out every night. Plus having to get ready for the show. Then finding Robin..." He trailed off.

Len spoke before JB could. "I don't get it. How can

you be too exhausted to paint? You stand in front of an easel and dab colors on a canvas. That's the US Medical Association's recommended cure for exhaustion."

Jathan became defensive. "All right. I haven't painted recently. So kill me. There are plenty of paintings here for me to use at the show. Work no one has seen. Why is everyone picking on me all the time? Why don't you just butt out? Both of you." He angrily turned and went back to the couch, sitting down with his back to them. Acting much like a huffy child.

JB leaned to Len and said, "This isn't going to be the least bit productive anymore. He's slipped into terrible tantrum mode again. I think our only choice right now is to do what he wants. Let's go."

Len nodded. But before they left Len went over to the couch. He bent so he was level with Jathan, leaned forward, and gave him a kiss on the cheek. Jathan shrank from the gesture. He was still angry. Standing, Len said, "When you get sick of being sick all the time come talk to me." He turned to JB. "Come on. Let's go. He'll get it or he won't. I've done what I could."

JB grabbed his coat, and as he followed Len out the door he turned back. "Jathan, really, I wish you good luck with your show."

※※※

Len came in to their apartment building lobby first. He went to JB's door and leaned against the jam, waiting.

JB followed a minute or two later, having stopped to let Sweets do her business. He reached into his pocket for his keys, stopped at the mail kiosk, and opened his box. He pulled out a stack of letters and shifting them, checked through them.

"Bills...and junk mail. That's why I don't check everyday. Doesn't anyone ever send personal letters anymore?"

"Well, there's this." Len held out an eleven by fourteen manila envelope. It had been left at JB's door. JB took it and looked at the address.

"Hand delivered, JB? Fancy, huh?"

"Its from Starzy. It must be the script she had written for that movie of hers. She said she'd send it over as soon as she had it." He opened the door. "I'll look at it later."

"Why not now? Aren't you the least bit curious? It wouldn't kill you to do it now."

"Now we don't know that do we."

"Well, it could be arranged…" Len followed JB inside.

Chapter 19

IT WAS MOVIE night at JB's place. Since Monday was Len's day off from the theater, the two of them had taken to renting a couple of movies and watching them that night. This week it was Len's turn to pick the films. JB supplied the popcorn. Major movies had been coming out on tape within a few months lately so Len had rented the recent *About Last Night,* a Demi Moore vehicle, and, as second choice, *The Golden Child.*

Never a big Eddie Murphy fan—the anti-gay and homophobic rants that filled his comedy act were a complete mystery to JB. He just didn't get it. Why would one minority person feel the need to attack and insult another minority? Was Murphy just being stupid or was he being malicious?—when Len slid the movie into the machine JB picked up the script Starzy had sent over. He fazed out the movie and concentrated on the story they had built from of his second book.

Scene one. Fade in...

Two hours later JB had read the one-hundred and twenty page script twice. He was, for lack of a more descriptive word, incredulous. Disbelief was the only viable emotion he could feel at what he held in his hands.

"So, what did you think?" Len asked as he hit the stop button on the VCR remote.

"Shocked. Horrified. Gobsmacked."

"I know you don't like Eddie Murphy, JB, but it wasn't that bad."

"Not that. This." He held up the script.

"You read it?"

"I was numbed by it."

"What's wrong?"

"What isn't wrong? For one thing you're no longer Len. You're Linda, a bosomy sex-starved assistant in love with Jace Bonner. That's me. I'm now a macho hard-drinking asswipe along the lines of a Mickey Spillane rip-off. Tristin is now named Calliope, a bimbo much like Goldie Hawn was on *Laugh-In*, with the giggles and all that other shit. About the only thing that hasn't been changed is the dog...and Lisa. Even the little girl is now fourteen and a nubile *Lolita*. The play device has totally disappeared. Toby has disappeared..." JB threw the script down on the coffee table. "It's an absolute shambles."

"What did you expect? Its Hollywood."

"That's no excuse for eviscerating the entire novel. That is garbage, Len."

"Have they paid you yet? Has the check been cashed?"

"Well, yes."

"Then it really isn't any of your business what they've done with it, is it? You gave them the rights. Complete and utter. They can do anything they want. Make paper dolls out of it if they please."

"That's basically what they've done, Len. This script has absolutely no relation to any sort of good or decent moviemaking I've ever seen. Its slick, exploitative, superficial shit...complete with exploding cars."

"But it will look terrific, I'll bet. You know the movies these days. They're all style over substance, and never considered completely worthless if they look fabulous. So don't get yourself all in a swivitt over it."

JB shook his head. "Huh? What was that? You know I love it when you pull out these old Southern expressions. What the hell is a swivitt?"

"A dither. Agitated. Sweating over small stuff."

He handed over a sheet of paper to Len. "Then that is something to get a swivitt about."

"You don't 'get a' you 'get into'. So, what are you swivitting about now?"

"That's a proposed cast list. Look at the lead."

"Starzy?"

"Male lead."

"Oh. Kirk Hazzard?" Len shrugged. "Maybe a bit old for the part, but he's competent...not exactly Harrison Ford as *Indiana Jones*, but okay. He's still box office."

"Well, we hate him. And I won't stand for him playing a character that's based on me."

"Enough for you to give up all the money? You'll have to give it all back, you know, if you object to anything? Wasn't that what the contract said?"

"It was, and I don't care. I refuse to let that asshole play in my movie."

"For God's sake, why? And must I remind you again; it isn't your movie. What in heaven's name do you have against Kirk Hazard?"

"It was years ago. I was a kid. Brand new to New York. Still wide-eyed by it all. I'd seen Hazzard in my first Broadway play just a few days before. Okay, I was star struck, but there he was, standing on the street, trying to hail a cab. I didn't want to look like a total rube so I went up to him and asked directions to the subway. He didn't even look. He just said, 'Fuck off, kid. Do I look like a Goddamned traffic cop?' I've disliked the man ever since. He snubbed me, Len. I just can't stand him. Besides, he's really a lousy actor. I've hated every movie he's ever done."

"And from such small incidents careers are made...or splashed like turds into the porcelain facility. Edith Piaf was right."

"What?"

"She said one should be careful who you cross on the way up, because the same people are waiting for you on the way back down. Or something to that effect. And it applies here." JB was bemused. "Hazard didn't know you or that you'd have this kind of power over him all these years later. So he acted like a jerk back then. And you've never forgotten. Or forgiven, it would seem. Now you hold this plum part in your writhing little hands." Len circled a finger and pointed skyward. "Revenge!', cried the Count of Monte Cristo."

"Not quite so dramatic as all that, but I see your point. I can give him the part or take it away."

"You know, if the script is really as bad as you say it is..."

"It's so bad I'll need to hire a stable boy to clean up the mess it's made."

"Then wouldn't a really execrable movie do more damage to his career than not getting the part? How many actors have scuttled their careers because of bad choices? Wouldn't it hurt far more for Mr. Hazard to actually get the part?" He laughed a theatrically sinister, "Mawha, ha, ha, ha."

"Humm. I get you. I swear, Len Matthews, you truly are the demonic spawn of Stan."

"Don't you mean Satan?"

"No. I mean Stan. Stan was this evil queen that lived next door to me when I was in the Village. He's not Satan by any means, but by most gay standards he's pretty rude."

Len laughed.

JB thought a moment then said, "I'll have to think about all this some more. Meanwhile, I do have to go see Starzy." He indicated the script. "To return that piece of flotsam if nothing else."

Chapter 20

STARZY WASN'T LIVING at the Algonquin Hotel anymore. She had, instead, found an actor friend who was going out of town and taken a six month sublet on his place up in the East eighties.

The morning after movie night JB put Sweets on her newly purchased black leather leash and walked her the twenty or so blocks over to Starzy's building off

Second Avenue, ostensibly to return the script she had sent him. His real purpose was to tell her he'd decided, as Len had proposed, to offer absolutely no constructive ideas or remedies for her script. Especially since his only truthful suggestion would be to throw the entire mess into the East River and let it drown. He felt that as long as his name was nowhere to be seen on any of the film's publicity or title sequences anything they did would be okay with him. Let them sink into the mire of *Ishtar, Heaven's Gate,* and *Howard's Duck* all on their lonesome.

He rang the bell at her apartment door, there being no doorman or outside security for the three story walk-up building. He made a note to himself to mention that it wasn't the safest way to live in New York City. It wouldn't hurt if she got a few extra locks for her door as extra protection.

She didn't answer right away, so JB rang again, then knocked. This time there was the sound of a lock being unlatched and a chain being slid into place. It sounded like at least a couple of safety measures were there already. The door opened a crack. Starzy's eye and a bit of cheek appeared.

"Oh, hi, JB. I wasn't expecting you," she said softly. Her voice, normally happy if not sliding dangerously into perky, sounded now as if she might be ill or in pain. That was when JB noticed a rather ugly red bruise at the side of her lip. What the hell? Next he spied an open gash at her eyebrow that didn't look good at all. It was about two inches long with dried blood crusted at its center and deep red going to purple bruising around its perimeter.

"What's happened to you, Starzy? You don't look well. Let me in. Maybe I can help." She was all set to say no, but JB wouldn't hear of it. "Come on, hon. None of that. Open up. You've been hurt. I can see it. Let me help."

She mummered an okay and shut the door. He could hear her removing an iron safety bar, opening a couple of bolts, and sliding the chain off. It was obvious she had more than enough locks already on her door. Any security advice he might offer wouldn't be required.

She opened the door an inch, leaving it for him to enter as she limped on a bad leg toward the living room. She was in bad shape, that much was clear. Her right arm was in a sling she had fashioned from a scarf and she was holding her shoulder stiffly, as if it might be sprained, or worse, dislocated. JB could also see one or two smaller cuts on her face, a split lip on the side of her face he hadn't been able to see at the door, and another nasty gash at her right hairline staining a bloody blackish circle onto her white blond hair.

Her limping so slowly toward the couch meant JB was able to catch up to her easily after he had secured the door and tied Sweets to the knob. He put an arm around her to help, but took it away quickly when she sucked in air, as if he might have hurt her in some way. JB suspected there might be a broken rib at fault. He helped her to lie down on the couch, offered to get her a cup of hot tea or some kind of pain medication, then couldn't hold his curiosity back any longer. He sat tentatively on the edge of the couch facing her, "Tell me what happened?"

She opened her eyes and through her swollen lips said one word, "Mugged." Then she moaned.

"Damn. You were mugged? Where?" JB looked around the apartment. The scene of the crime became instantly clear. The place was a mess. And was obviously the site of her attack. Overturned furniture gave proof to what had happened, and a rounded dent in the plaster wall where a head had smashed into it testified to the violence of it. "Here?" JB asked. "In this apartment? There was an invasion?"

Starzy nodded. "He broke in. Beat me. Robbed me. Awful." A tear ran down her cheek.

"A man. Who? Did you know him?" She shook her head. "When did this happen."

"Not long. Few hours ago."

"Then you haven't been looked at have you? You

need to see a doctor."

"No," she said, and managed to sit up. She put her hand on JB's arm. "Can't. The publicity..."

JB stood and looked for the phone. "Starzy, you need to be looked at by a professional. We'll come up with something to keep the newspaper jackals away. Don't worry about it."

She moaned again and lay back down. JB found the phone on the floor, a faint undulating tone sounding from the receiver. He put it back onto the cradle, waited a second, picked it back up, got a dial tone, and punched in nine-one-one.

※ ※ ※

Paramedics arrived within ten minutes and carried Starzy on a stretcher to their waiting van. JB rode with her to the nearest emergency room where they checked her in as Agnes Gooch—using a character from *Auntie Mame* to keep any reporters at bay—then JB waited while the staff took over.

She did, indeed, have a broken rib. Plus a dislocated shoulder, a sprained ankle, and the obvious cuts and bruises JB had seen before. The intruder had taken a major toll on her, causing injuries that would take some time to heal. That he had assaulted without raping her was a lucky break. She was going to be in some pain for several weeks to come. Once the emergency room staff fixed, stitched, and bandaged her, she was given a prescription for a strong pain medication, a sedative, and a bed. The hospital was keeping her overnight for observation.

Nurses, doing their duty, had reported the attack to the hospital police. A young woman in a uniform soon arrived to take Starzy's and JB's statements. Unfortunately for New York City, robbery and assault, muggings and attacks, were routine events, so the officer's interest was perfunctory at best. She took a report that would be filed and forgotten and left the ER soon after. But Starzy—with a considerable amount of drugs to dull the pain—and a mirror to see what her intruder had actually done to her, wasn't having it. She was exhibiting a righteous biblical sort of anger toward her attacker. An anger embroidered and stitched with bitterness and revenge fantasies. It was an old fashioned kind of angry. White hot and purple with her fury. A frontier angry. The kind that gathers the townsfolk to go out and hunt down the varmint so they can string him up kind of anger. How exactly she was going to accomplish this in modern day Manhattan JB didn't even want to contemplate.

Since medical staff was looking sfter Starzy she was now drowsy and falling asleep from the pills they had given her. JB checked his watch, and seeing that it was starting to get late—and, quite honestly, because JB was very discomfited by Starzy's ugly black mood—he decided not to stick around. He needed to get back to Starzy's apartment to pick up Sweets anyway, so he gave the floor nurse his home number and left the hospital.

※※※

The next afternoon both JB and Len picked up flowers from a close by market and went to the hospital to visit with Starzy. She was already sitting up in her bed and, more like her old sweeter self, was begging for her release. The hospital insisted she would need someone to accompany her or they couldn't let her go. Liability reasons or some such nonsense. So JB and Len were designated caretakers, and soon abetted Ms. Gooch's escape. She was back in disguise with a scarf over her head and dark glasses while they rolled her in a wheelchair to the hospitals main entrance. They flagged a cab, piled in, and had it take them back to her apartment.

Once there they helped her to bed, gave her the medication prescribed by her doctor, a cup of chamomile tea, and then left when she fell asleep soon after.

As they were walking back to their own building, Len said, "Okay, Nurse Ratchett, you have that look. What's gotten up your nose?"

"I don't know. Something just doesn't feel right about all this."

"Oh, good lord, you're at it again. Well, welcome to Suspicion Island. Population...you. Really, JB? The poor woman was brutally attacked in her own home. A person isn't safe anywhere anymore."

"And that's exactly it, Len. Exactly what's bothering me about all this." He grinned. "You really are getting good at putting your finger on the exact thing that doesn't fit. I'm very impressed."

Len beamed. Flattery, always an actor's nectar, and for Len one of life's vital fluids, was a quick and easy way to stop him from making his usual tacky remarks, always disparaging JB's flights of investigative inquisitiveness.

"What you're saying then, Len, is Starzy was safe in her apartment, right? She had locks, chains, even a safety bar on her door." He paused. "So, I ask you, then how did the burglar break in? There's no choice but to conclude that Starzy must have let him in." JB held up a hand, stopping Len from speaking. "I know exactly what you're going to ask. Why would she do that?"

"I'm not so sure about that, but..." Len by now was totally engaged with JB in the problem they were working on. "...I do have an idea why she might have let someone in. She'd ordered food. A pizza, maybe? The attacker was dressed as a delivery man. What would it take JB? A white napkin at his waist and a baseball cap. She'd open her door for that, wouldn't she? It's possible, isn't it?"

"Actually that is a possibility. A very good one. It would explain it, anyway. You really are getting good at this. I'll going to have to listen to you more often after this..."

They continued walking to their building.

It did explain it, JB was thinking, but it still wasn't the whole explanation he was looking for. He couldn't have explained it to Len, but there was some instinct at work. JB was finding he had this ability that told him when something felt right. Or it didn't. He had found a kind of heightened BS meter in his head, and it was proving very useful. It often gave him impressions about people he met. Was that one a phony? Or just an asshole? Was the fast talking one a crook? Or an enthusiast? Despite the sarcasm he was exhibiting was that one really a mensch? So far this impulse of his had been proving right. He'd always considered himself a fair judge of character, now that same trait was telling him he didn't have all he needed to put Starzy's attack aside. He'd have to talk to her again. After she'd recuperated some.

Chapter 21

DESPITE VARIOUS TRIES over the next week JB never did get to have that talk he wanted with Starzy. An interview with an *Advocate* reporter, a summons from his editor for a meeting, laundry, grocery shopping...life. They all intervened to keep them from seeing each other.

And then it somehow had become the next Sunday and JB remembered the invitation to Jathan's latest art show tacked onto his refrigerator door. He was sure that Starzy would be there, with her fading bruises covered by a layer of makeup, so he'd try to get her aside that evening. His invitation stated *"and guest"* so he called Len at the theater and asked him if he wanted to get dinner and attend the show after his matinee was done for the day.

They decided to go to the *Cottonwood Café* for dinner. Located in the Village on Beekman off Bank, it served old fashioned down home Tex-Mex comfort food. It was the first of its kind in New York until then. Chicken fried steak, mashed potatoes with skins, fried okra, and buttered cornbread were the restaurant's specialties. It was all priced ridiculously high, but many displaced Texans and Midwesterners would crave the gravy swamped taste of home and willingly paid the twenty dollars a plate, all the while knowing that it could be had back home for less than seven.

Finished with dinner JB and Len wandered, on foot, over toward Soho — so named because the area was SOuth of HOuston Street — and the Margo Greene Gallery. How Jathan had managed a show in so short a time — when most art galleries were booked several months, sometimes years, in advance — came up for discussion.

"Easily answered," Len said. "The business that was next door to her gallery went bust. Margo stepped in, quick like, and took over the store front. She's cut a couple of archways between the two spaces and now has doubled her hanging area with an annex. That new space is where she has Jathan showing."

They arrived at the gallery and showed their invitation to the man at the door. He checked his clipboard and finding JB's name passed them through. Inside they went to the coat check and handed over their outer garments, getting a paper chit from the girl in return.

The Margo Greene Gallery was far fancier than Jathan's previous showcase. For one thing, the wine being served was a superior California vintage with a choice of red or white. The food was laid out as a buffet and manned by jacketed waiters standing behind the cloth covered tables, while other waiters wandered the floor picking up finished plates and glasses and offering refills. The guests were a specially picked group of mid level A-list names straight out of the social pages, all dressed up in their best name designer finery. There were a few Rockefeller relatives, a couple of cousins from the Kennedy clan, and a mix of new guard and old guard celebrities. A Fonda, Dina Merrill (who breached both sides by being a well-known actress and a member of the Kellogg dynasty), Steve Martin, along with the required "whales" that kept a gallery going. These were the collectors, often with more money than taste, who could afford to spend large amounts on art. All in all it was a giant step up from where Jathan had started in the Manhattan subways.

The gallery featured off white plain walls, with hanging aluminum grids of lights picking out the framed pieces hung along them. Three half walls down the center kept the first gallery from being simply an open hanger. An exposed brick wall with two angled archways cut into them separated one space from the other. The second space—where Jathan's art was showing—was a narrow open gallery. Polished hardwood floors ran through both spaces causing high-heels and wing tips to make clicking and clacking noises as the crowd milled around the paintings.

Apparently having learned his lesson, Jathan was already there, standing at the far end of the second gallery, a cocktail in one hand, a cigarette in the other, with one of his larger pieces back framing him. He was pushing the outsider image he was trying to effect by wearing a vintage Forties white dinner jacket and black tux trousers. What made it outré was that he was bare chested under the coat. That caused some talk—which was what he was going for—and got him approving titters from some of the younger female contingent. He was basking in the attention he was gathering from the crowd, who were standing around him listening raptly to whatever BS he was passing out. Ego, how you have blossomed and grown in these fertile fields.

Margo Greene, going Jathan one better in the outrageous fashion department, was standing at the front of the space trying to get everyone's attention by tinking a fork against a flute. In her mid fifties, she was dressed in all black, with a long satin skirt split to the knee and a wide lapeled jacket, all enhanced by multitudes of silver safety pins, creating designs similar to English buskers over it. Her hair was dyed black with orange tips and cut in sharp angles, giving it an architectural slant. Her squinty myopic eyes peered out from behind giant round framed yellow tinted glasses. She was a character and her look was as much a part of her success as the art she showed. Her own reputation had been made when she was in the vanguard of the late Fifties by showing Jasper Johns, Marcel Duchamp and Max Ernst. More recently, in the Seventies, she'd made a splash by showing Robert Mapplethorpe's homoerotic photographs. She was hoping to strike paydirt again with Jathan's illustrative graffiti paintings.

Finally getting everyone's attention she started a rambling speech, in her trademark little girl voice, which covered the last twenty years of her career. Eventually, it was presumed by all, she would get to the part about Jathan and his new work where she would formally introduce him to the public as her latest art wunderkind.

It also appeared that Jathan wasn't having it. Breaking all the rules of decorum he started to come forward from the back of the gallery toward Margo. He was even pushing people aside to do so. It looked as if he was going to live up to that bad boy image he'd been working on after all. At least that was what was believed by most of the guests as they watched him come on, step by step, toward Margo. Believed that is, until a woman he'd just gone past gasped and pointed. Her gesture drew attention to the possibility of there being something not okay about him. Which caused the crowd to begin mumbling amongst themselves. What was it? What's wrong? What's going to happen?

What happened was the guests began to back away, clearing a path for Jathan as he continued advancing on the now silenced Margo. What seemed odd to those watching was his gait. He wasn't striding or ambling to the front, he was lumbering. His legs were wobbly, almost seeming unable to hold him upright. And he wasn't moving in a straight line, he was lurching and weaving like some character out of a Hollywood horror movie. The Mummy stalking his victim. It was almost comical and a few of the guests chuckled. Was that it? Was he making fun of Margo by parodying a movie monster? What was he thinking?

He kept coming forward until he was about ten feet away from Margo. He stopped there as the bones in his knees seemed to dissolve, and down he went. He reached an arm out to her, his fingers grasping at the air. She cringed and stepped back, rightfully fearful and not at all sure of the situation. Then Jathan fell forward and landed face down on the floor. The reason was then quickly explained by a thin bladed knife protruding from between his shoulder blades, red blood staining the pure white of his jacket.

A collective gasp went around the room. Jathan turned on his side as JB and Len both moved to him. They knelt beside him. Len called out, "Someone call an ambulance. Now!" Jathan took hold of JB's arm, using it as a lever, and lifted himself slightly. His eyes were wide saucers of fear and anguish. In the now hushed room he said one word, "Starzy..."

"I'm here, sweetheart." She stepped out from the crowd, and rushed to his side. Bending beside him she took hold of his hand, "It'll be all right. I know it will. Won't it JB? Say it will be all right..." She sounded on the very edge of hysteria, keeping herself in check only so Jathan, or more likely herself, wouldn't fall over the edge into outright crazy.

JB was a bit surprised at seeing her, as he hadn't realized that Starzy was even in the gallery —

he hadn't spotted her when they'd come in. And he should have seen her considering she was wearing a silver sequined and chiffon cocktail outfit with strappy shoes to match. She would have stood out. She must have been somewhere out of his sight. But now here she was comforting her brother as he lay wounded, her eyes beseeching JB to back up her most fervent wish. He felt he couldn't speak to the truth of her hope, but nodded in sympathy, then stood back, watching the two of them.

Behind him two women, one wearing a Nolan Miller gown with his ubiquitous football player shoulder pads and spangles, the other in a Halston jersey draped column, spoke between themselves.

"Oh, dear, it looks as if he was stabbed," said the Nolan Miller lady.

"Unbelievable. And I must have seen the killer..." the other lady added.

JB spun to face the women. "You did? What was it you saw? Exactly? Tell me."

His command must have taken the two of them by surprise because they gasped at JB's abrupt tone. These women were far more used to giving orders than taking them. "It's very important, ladies. I need to know what you saw."

The Halston lady spoke first. "Well, I didn't see much. I was standing back there with Miffy Stewart..." She turned to her friend. "You know her, dear. You met her at Rocky's Easter soirée." Her friend nodded.

JB insisted, "Will you please focus, ma'am. Where were you?"

She straightened her back. "Well," she huffed. Then she pointed to where Jathan had come from. To the back of the gallery. "I was there. I saw him stiffen and start coming to the front."

"Was anyone with him? Was there anyone else?"

"There was a woman moving away from him. So, she wasn't really with him, so to speak. That was all I saw," she finished, dismissing JB by turning to face her friend.

But JB wasn't going to let it go. "The woman. Which direction was she going? To the outside? To the right?"

She turned her head back to JB. "No, toward that wall over there. To the left."

"Could you see her. Describe her?"

Now she was simply bored with his questioning. Her voice took on the tone he was sure she reserved for servants and peons. Leona Helmsley had nothing on this dame.

"She was in black. Wearing a bulky coat, with a flowered skirt. Daytime street clothing. Highly inappropriate for the occasion. Oh, and a scarf. Wrapped like a babushka around her head. And large sunglasses. The kind Jackie wears. You know the type don't you, dear?" Her friend nodded again. "Her coat had its collar pulled up, so I couldn't see her face clearly. She seemed Slavic somehow. Polish maybe. We saw many like her when we were in Prague last year. But you know what Prague is like?" She turned to her friend. "So much like New York, dear, but still with some remnants of whimsy about it." Her friend nodded once again.

"The police are going to want to know everything you've just told me. They should be here shortly."

An ambulance siren could be heard approaching, and slightly behind that a different toned siren wailed. That would be the police, JB was betting.

The guests were all herded willingly into the other side of the gallery, away from Jathan's body, by the staff. They milled about in a flashy cluster waiting for something to happen. There was an aura of expectant excitement while they waited. These people weren't witness to a murder every day.

They then had to make way for a set of paramedics as a stretcher was rolled to where Jathan was lying. One man on each side, they lifted him and strapped him onto the gurney. Starzy stayed beside him holding his hand. The lifting must have caused some sort of trauma because Jathan gripped Starzy's hand hard, took a heavy breath, exhaled, and went limp.

"He's in respiratory arrest. Let's get him out of here..." one of the medics shouted to the other. They quickly rolled the gurney toward the door.

"Oh, no. No," Starzy cried out. She was left standing alone, her hands covering her face, sobs racking her body. Len went to her, took her by the shoulders and walked her to a nearby bench, where she collapsed against his chest.

JB followed the paramedics out to the ambulance. He watched as they got Jathan inside and began practicing their life saving efforts on him.

※※※

While this was all happening the police had also arrived at the gallery. A couple of NYPD cruisers pulled up, headlights glaring, their sirens winding down, as they parked catty corner on the street. They piled out of their cars and began to secure the area by running yellow police tape between lampposts and waste bins and moving the small crowd that had gathered away from the immediate vicinity.

A plain clothes detective came over to the ambulance. He was clearly the one who going to be in charge. He was named O'Dowd according to the plastic strip attached to his coat pocket. He was middle-aged, pasty, unhealthy looking, and overweight. He looked as if he'd need a boomerang to put on his belt. Like most cops he'd seen these situations before. This was plainly just one more to him.

Between the medics and JB it was soon explained to him what had happened. Detective O'Dowd then took over, beginning by directing his men to various stations inside the gallery to start taking statements. Others were dispatched to keep control of the area. JB had a discussion with the detective for several minutes, then returned to the gallery himself.

※※※

Once back inside, he went immediately to where Len and Starzy were still sitting on a bench in the second gallery. Starzy reached for JB's hand, gripping it hard in her worry over Jathan's condition.

"He's still alive. They saved him, Starzy. They used a defibrillator on him and got his heart started. He's unconscious but alive. They're taking him to the Downtown Hospital right now."

"Then I have to go to him." Starzy stood and started to head for the front.

"You can't, Starzy. The police will need to get your statement first. You'll have to wait."

She sat back down and with Len waited. JB didn't stay with them. Instead he went to the back of the gallery, where all of this had started. He was meaning to check out what the two women had told him earlier.

He stood where Jathan had been and looked to his left, where the Halston lady had said the woman she'd seen had fled. There was a swinging door on that wall. JB went to it and pushed. He leaned in when it opened.

Behind it was a long hallway, going the length of the building. He could also see there were open doorways along the outer side of the hall. It all had the look of new construction, undoubtedly from Margo Greene recently taking over the space. Unpainted walls with taped and spackled seams. Bare concrete floors. Unframed doorjambs. Signs of the continuing construction on the space. Margo had only managed to get the place presentable in the public areas; the rest was obviously still being finished. As JB walked down the hall he found the doorways were entrances to various rooms. Storage spaces and offices mostly. He passed a small kitchen where two members of the catering staff were cleaning up, and a lounge area where that evenings waiters sat waiting for the cops to get to them. The back rooms explained why the second gallery was so slender—they had cut these utilitarian spaces out of the whole.

When JB got to the far end of the hallway he had to make a sharp left. That led him to the back end of the front cloak room. At the other end of that was the entrance to the main gallery. Where he and Len had handed in their coats when they'd first come in. He walked the length of the narrow room and leaned out over the half door at the front.

It was clear that this was the way the attacker had escaped notice. It provided a perfect exit out through the front while the guests were crowded in the second gallery watching Jathan's distress. But JB wasn't accepting it. He wasn't going to be content with so simple an explanation. There was more to this than met anyone's eye.

JB turned back and checked out the cloak room. Plainly built and constricting in width it only provided room for racks with coats on one side and just enough space to move along the edge of it to retrieve or hang them on the other. He went back to the rear of the room and bending down started duck walking his way back to the front. Midway along he stopped, reached under the hanging garments and pulled out a bundle he had found stashed there. Opening it he saw what he had expected to find. He rewrapped it and returned it to where he'd found it, stood, and then went off to find Detective O'Dowd.

As he walked through the gallery he spotted the woman he had talked with earlier. The lady wearing the Halston gown. He stopped and sat beside her to ask her a few more questions. But she, doing her own impression of Queen Victoria, was not amused at him intruding on her once again. She turned to her companion, her back to JB, effectively cutting him off. She was determined to ignore him. This wouldn't do, he realized. Not at all.

JB stood up and went looking again. This time, instead of looking for the detective, he wanted Len. He found him cruising one of the waiters.

He called him over. "What are you doing?"

"That boy there. He was giving me signals."

"What? With fire and a blanket? Right now I need your expertise. Come on."

"Where?"

"I'll explain as we go."

※※※

When Len went up to the Halston woman she recognized him right away. She also quite suddenly became graciousness personified. Celebrity. Shazam! You got what you wanted. Like getting table's in restaurants and preferential treatment at events you attend. It was a fact of life, people want to curry favor from the famous. Len Matthews was famous. Ergo, he usually got what he wanted. It had worked its magic one more time. Len sat beside her and smiled his most winning smile.

"You were previously so helpful to my friend." He indicated JB who was standing a little bit away. "I was wondering if we could impose upon you once more?" Len could be a master at smoothing ruffled sensibilities when he wanted to. Like butter melting on an English muffin he was. Now, sufficiently flattered, the woman nodded her agreement. "Thank you so much, dear lady." He shifted and waved JB over.

JB moved in and sat next to her. "You were so marvelously observant before..." JB could slather a bit of margarine himself when it was needed. Quickly getting to his point, he asked, "I was wondering if you noticed anything else about that woman you saw?"

※※※

Finished with his last minute questions with the Halston gowned women JB and Len were headed to the front of the main gallery in search of the detective in charge.

"By the way, where's Starzy?" JB asked. "I thought you were with her."

"I presume she's on her way to the hospital to check on Jathan. She was pretty worried about him. We waited together until the officer took her statement, then that gorgeous waiter man came upon my gaydar. I have to admit I wasn't paying much attention to Starzy after he showed up. He was way too delicious on the eye.

"I swear, Len, God gave you a penis and a brain, and only enough blood to run one of them at a time."

"Humph. You know if I really wanted to hear from an ass I could just fart. So there. You're not the only one who can be fast with a good line."

"Actually, I think I might be, Len. So Starzy just up and left?"

"When I was chatting up the waiter fellow. Wasn't she supposed to?"

"We need to talk to Detective O'Dowd. Right away. Come on."

Chapter 22

THE ICU HOSPITAL room was morbidly quiet, the dark cut only by a rectangle of light shining on the floor from the hallway outside. Lights flashing and oscilloscopes beeping from electrocardiogram and electroencephalogram machines standing by the bed made the only sounds. That is until the click of a pair of high heels could be heard making their way down the hallway outside.

Expecting them to pass by the room on the way to another location, JB was nevertheless only mildly surprised when they stopped at the door of his room. He shifted in the bed and pulled the blanket covering him higher up on his neck.

Standing in the doorway was what most anyone would have guessed was a nurse. She was dressed in a set of standard green scrubs and held a metal tray in her hands. A nurse seeing to her patient. Since she was backlighted by light from the outside hall, her front was in shadow — her face only a dark blur.

She paused for a moment, then stepped into the room. She set her tray down on the table beside the bed and went to work. She began to prepare a syringe by filling it with the fluid from a small bottle. Then she paused long enough to test it. A flick of her finger against the glass tube to break up any bubbles, then a thin stream of the liquid squirting from the needle's eye caught the light coming in from the doorway. She turned to face the bed and picked out one of the plastic tubes hanging from the bedside post, slipped the hypodermic needle into the tube, and lifted her thumb —ready to plunge down on the shaft of the syringe, forcing the liquid into the tube.

JB reached up and switched on the light over the bed.

"It won't work, Starzy," he said quietly, making his voice as full of understanding as he could muster considering she was trying to kill him.

She started, dropped the tube and stepped back. Now that she could be seen she didn't look at all like the star she was always photographed as. She wore no makeup and had on a short brown wig and glasses that were meant to obscure her eyes. They now looked at JB wide open in shock. Which instantly morphed into pure rage. She growled a guttural screech at him and stepped to the bed. Her arms lifted above her head. She was going to plunge the syringe needle straight into JB's chest.

He quickly reached up and grabbed her wrists,

holding on to her as she twisted and turned trying to break his grip. She growled again. Then she started to scream a litany of obscenities at him, at the room, at her predicament, at the unfair world.

JB shouted, "Len, will you do something! Act like a cop and get this hellion away from me."

Len switched on the overhead lights, flooding the room with bright fluorescence. "The only thing I've ever done resembling a cop is to put on a pair handcuffs and say 'Do you know how fast you were going.' But, I suppose I can do this."

He placed two fingers to his lips and whistled. A shrill piercing sound that would have stopped a cab out on the street. It brought the desk nurse running. Also, moments later, it brought two uniformed cops and Detective O'Dowd rushing in to take Starzy by the waist and pull her away from JB.

They had her sitting in a chair and handcuffed in seconds. She thrashed from side to side, already claiming her innocence. "I didn't do anything. Nothing. You can't keep me here…"

Denial is a river in Egypt.

※※※

It had taken JB and Len only a minute to find the lead detective standing in the main art gallery. Officer O'Dowd was by the door watching as one of the Rockerfeller couples departed. "More money than sense, I swear," he said for no one to hear. He shook his head.

JB stepped up to stand beside him. "Detective, I was wondering if I could have some of your time. I need to show you something."

He turned to face JB. "What are you up to? You haven't disturbed anything have you?"

"There's something you need to see. Right over there." He pointed to the cloak room door. "I'll take you to it."

JB waved a hand to get the officer to follow him. He took him into the closet, then directed him to the bundle he'd found earlier.

"I left it alone, detective, thinking you would want to see it in situ." Where before hanging garments had hid it, now that most of the gallery guests had left, it was plainly visible.

The cop picked it up. "So what is this?"

"It's the killer's disguise. What was worn when Jathan was stabbed."

The cop started to carry the bundle back to the front, which caused JB to walk backward to get out of his way. As he did he ran into Len, who was standing at the door.

"What are you doing, JB? You're supposed to come out of closets, not stand in them."

"Coming out of the closet is something you only do once, Len. Like being born or sitting through *Cats*. I did it years ago."

Once they were all out in the lobby again O'Dowd laid the bundle down and untied the arms of a coat to release the articles inside. There was a flowered cotton skirt, a cheap patterned satin scarf, and a pair of round rimmed glasses.

JB explained. "It was worn to cover up who the attacker really was. She had done it before. With me."

"Wait. How do you know the attacker was a woman?"

"Well the skirt for one thing."

Len piped up. "Maybe it was a transvestite who attacked Jathan? With abysmal taste it looks like. That skirt with that scarf? Ugh."

"And maybe you should shut your hole if you aren't going to help."

Len hurumped but remained quiet for the moment.

JB told O'Dowd what the Halston woman had said to him. Then added, "On further reflection, she remembered that the woman who was dressed like a Polish refugee was also wearing silver high heel shoes."

"Totally out of place with that outfit," Len said. "Tre tacky."

JB stared at him. "O...kay."

Then he finished what he was saying to the detective. "The woman said the shoes were strappy little things with a rhinestone trim."

'Which was exactly the kind of shoes that Starzy Hillard was wearing to match her dress," Len added sarcastically. "Does that help, JB?" The cop stared at him much the same way that JB had. "I notice those kinds of things. So kill me."

"He's right. It was Starzy. What she did was put those clothes on so she could masquerade as some unknown person. Anyone who saw her would think she was only an ill dressed fan of the artist. You do know that most assailants are known to their victims, right?"

The detective nodded and indicated JB should go on.

"After the attack, Starzy used the hallway that runs along the second gallery to make her way to the cloak room. She took off the disguise, threw it under the coat racks, and moments later was leaning down next to Jathan consoling him. She probably meant to come back later to retrieve her disguise."

"Then you're saying that Starzy Hillard, the movie star, attacked Jathan Holt, the artist. Am I getting this right."

"Exactly. And furthermore, she knows that Jathan is still alive."

Len grabbed JB's arm. "And she's not here anymore."

JB said to the detective. "What do you want to bet she's on her way to the hospital to finish the job. She's going to kill him, detective."

"Not if we get there first."

The detective, even with his weight issues, was very quick on his feet. He was running off toward the outside, causing JB and Len to have to run to catch up with him. Outside, he went directly to one of the black and white cruisers parked there. He called to one of his officers to drive, and got into the front seat. JB and Len came up to the car door, panting.

"If you're coming get in the back," he barked. "Otherwise get out of the way."

The car motor turned over and the driver hit the gas, causing the engine to rev. They jumped in, slamming the back door as they did. With its siren blasting and the cruiser running past traffic and through red lights, they were at the Downtown Hospital in minutes. Hopefully ahead of Starzy.

※※※

JB was sitting on the bed talking at Starzy. "Nurses don't wear highheels to work in."

O'Dowd took over. "And that, ma'am, is part of the reason you are being charged tonight with murder and assault."

"What!, she shouted. "That's crazy. Goddamn it, who am I supposed to have murdered? Her face was crimson and screwed up ugly with her anger. Sputtering words because of her emotional state she blustered, "It sure as hell isn't this little thing with JB." She made a derisive sound. "It would be assault at most. Minor. Any lawyer could get me out of it with the turn of a writ."

JB huffed, "A syringe to the chest with whatever poison you put in there is more than assault. That's murderous intent. And that ain't some little charge, missy."

O'Dowd went on, "But Mr. Bent here would only be a secondary charge in your case. You're being charged with the first degree murder of Jathan Holt."

※※※

The police car skidded to a stop in front of the Emergency Room entrance. JB, Len, and O'Dowd piled out of the car like clowns at a Barnum and Bailey show, and aimed straight for the inside nurses station. Flashing his badge at the nurse behind the desk got her immediate attention, which soon gave O'Dowd the most recent information on Jathan.

It wasn't good. Jathan had died on the way

to the hospital. It turned out, after examination of the body, that the knife blade in his back had put a small nick on the rear of the heart. Although the paramedics had brought him back with their life saving electrical jolt, internal bleeding had caused him to expire before he reached the hospital. He was now lying downstairs in the morgue awaiting autopsy.

O'Dowd passed on the information to JB and Len, and added, "We won't be able to catch the Hillard woman getting to him after all. She won't try anything when she finds out he's already dead."

JB looked at O'Dowd slyly. "But she's not here yet, is she? So she doesn't know he's dead, does she? What if we could catch her in the act of trying to kill Jathan?"

"How do you propose we do that?"

"Is there a bed available in the ICU unit?"

※ ※ ※

Starzy was grasping at very thin straws.

"What if I said that Jathan wasn't really Jathan? Would that erase the murder charge?"

She was desperate, trying any maneuver she could to mitigate the charges. To bargain her way out of a death penalty. Her voice quivered as she looked for some sympathy. Any amount would do.

"He was the one who beat me, JB. He came to my apartment that day and battered me. Beat me. Abused me. You know, JB, you saw it. You helped me."

"I did. But why? Why would he beat you, Starzy?"

"Because I knew. I knew almost right away that he wasn't Jathan. He wasn't my Jay Nathan. I knew it was Robin, Detective. Jathan's twin. He'd killed Jay Nathan and tried to take over his life. But I was on to him. He wanted to make sure I wouldn't tell so he attacked me. To intimidate me. Don't you see? That's the reason I had to kill him. He was the real murderer. He killed Jay Nathan."

And she burst into sobs. Racking sobs that made her grab frantically for air. Panic, anxiety, realization at what she had done, relief at no longer keeping it all to herself, had caused her to break completely.

And it all fell into place for JB at that exact moment. Everything was explained. The puzzle was solved.

Why hadn't he seen it before? Now that he knew all of the facts it was all as clear as crystal. Robin was Jathan. Of course. Jathan was already dead. Well, duh.

That hadn't been Robin lying dead in Weatherwax's room that night, it was Jathan's body they had found. Robin killed his own twin brother, changed clothes with him, and had taken on his persona. Of course. He must have been planning to live the good life as a successful artist. It didn't matter that he couldn't paint or draw, there were racks full of Jathan's paintings he could sell until his own bank balance was bursting at the seams.

The clues were all there if JB had been looking. But he hadn't. He'd made the mistake of taking everything at its face value. He simply hadn't clicked on Jathan's wild behavior of late, putting it on the effects of fame. That newly found bad boy image that the papers propagated was Robin being the delinquent. Not Jathan.

Then JB remembered that after the killing Jathan had always called his adopted sister by her stage name, Starzy, not by her real name, Susan, or Suzy, as he had used when they'd first met. Robin wouldn't have known that was Jathan's habit, would he?

And what about Sweets and his mad barking at him that time they had visited? She had been friendly with Jathan before. Now her barking made sense. The dog had known it was Robin she was raging at—she'd known Robin from before, out in California. From when Weatherwax was alive and Robin was around her. As the photographs in Weatherwax's album had attested too—JB was sure that Sweets probably hadn't liked Robin. Maybe he'd abused her in some way? Beaten her? Dogs don't forget.

Also, hadn't Robin shrunk from Len's kiss that day? Would a gay man do that? Sure. If he was angry with Len, as he supposedly was. But a straight man certainly wouldn't want another man kissing at him. That was why Robin had looked so miserable in all those pictures with Weatherwax. Robin was hanging around with a gay man who was turned on to him, after him. Robin was probably using that misplaced affection to con Weatherwax into becoming his partner in crime. But Robin was a straight man, and not interested in other men as his sexual partners. So, of course, Weatherwax, and then Len, smooching at him would make him pull away.

Robin had needed a safe place to hide after he and Weatherwax had their falling out over the scams they'd been pulling. He'd killed Weatherwax in that store window and had to get away. He needed someplace to hide. What better way to hide in plain sight than by taking over someone else's life? Robin pretending to be Jathan gave him safe haven. That is until Starzy unmasked him. She could have ruined his perfect impersonation, so he went to her apartment and he beat her up. It was the way most thugs would handle such a problem, wasn't it? But Starzy didn't just roll over. She decided to take her own revenge. She wasn't going to let some imposter take over her brother's life.

※※※

"My...God...what...have...I...done..." Starzy moaned. She was already up to page thirty-seven of the Kübler-Ross Stages of Grief manual. She was at acceptance. She slumped in her chair, quietly staring ahead, belatedly realizing what her actions had brought about — to Robin, to her career, to her life. She had come to the realization that she was ruined, and faced a substantial time in prison, if not worse. It was going to be a first degree murder charge. It was over.

※※※

But JB, being the suspicious soul Len always accused him of, suspected there might be some other reason for Starzy to have taken Robin out. If that was the case then his killing wasn't only a matter of revenge. It was a planned and methodical pre-meditated murder for gain.

Weren't Jathan's paintings also a viable motive for her to kill? Wasn't it Starzy who would be the beneficiary of Jathan's estate with his brother now dead? Wouldn't she inherit all of his assets now? If she did she would have well over a hundred paintings by the hottest artist to hit the New York art scene in at least a decade. How much money would those paintings bring now that Jathan was deceased? It had to be a very big amount of moola considering what his works were already bringing in.

But why would she need it? Starzy had a Hollywood career of her own that stood to make her a very pretty penny, so why would she need Jathan's estate? Then again — as has been well documented — Hollywood careers can be notoriously short lived. Too many careers had been wrecked upon the shoals of bad movies and poor choices. And Starzy's movies hadn't been doing all that well at the box office lately. Also Starzy was going to be facing her dreaded thirties in only a few years. If she couldn't revive her acting career? — maybe she was looking to take care of what she saw as a wobbly and uncertain future.

JB wondered if, psychologically, there was enough rage inside the woman to drive her to inflict such violence on another person? JB had seen over the last few weeks that Starzy, sweet little narcissist that she appeared to be, would do whatever was needed to get what she wanted. As prime example, the manipulation she had pulled over the rights to his novel. Also there was her initial reaction to her beating. JB remembered that burning anger she had displayed that night at the hospital. Would it translate to enough anger to open the door and let in Death himself? Would her anger have festered and boiled inside her until it had no choice but to spew out in the ultimate violence?

※※※

O'Dowd was questioning Starzy. "So you're saying that you killed Robin Holt, not Jathan Holt, as payback for the beating he inflicted on you? And as revenge for his murdering your brother? Am I getting this right?"

Starzy sighed. "I don't think I want to say any more to you. I want a lawyer. Get me a lawyer and then we'll see what happens."

It looked to JB as if she wasn't going to make it easy for the police despite any accepting she may have done. Her lawyering up was simply a stop gap. A desperate way to delay the wheels from turning quite so quickly.

O'Dowd shook his head and said, "If that's the way you want it? Then I'm arresting you for the murder of..."

※※※

Len was standing by the door with JB watching Starzy being put in cuffs. He asked, "Are we so sure she did this, JB? She doesn't really seem crazy enough to kill anybody?"

"What a person seems and what they are capable of are two different things, Len. I was reading a psych book the other day..."

"Wait, you read psychology books for fun? We really have to do something about your social life, JB."

"I was reading about something called Intermittent Explosive Disorder."

"So she gets mad every once in a while?"

"IED is more than that. It's characterized by sporadic episodes of extreme aggression, violence, and destructive behavior. At least that's what the book said."

"It sounds like psychobabble for childish tantrums. In the good old days that would get you a severe spanking."

"You're advocating child abuse then? What you mean is back in the good old, incredibly disturbing, days."

"So, if she has this intermittent thing she could actually kill?"

"If she was under the influence of the disorder, at the mercy of her own anger, then yes, she could probably kill."

"Maybe you should tell Starzy about this, it sounds like one hell of a defense to me."

Chapter 23

STARZY DIDN'T REMAIN in police custody very long. A phalanx of lawyers showed up the next morning. They had her out and on a plane back to the West Coast before the day was over. She was going to end up hiding out in another state until her lawyers had exhausted every avenue they could to get the charges dropped. Or greatly reduced. Deals were flying back and forth as fast as modern telecommunications could carry them.

The next few weeks served to bring out even more information on the Starzy Night case, as it was coming to be called by the tabloids. *Entertainment Tonight*, the Hollywood gossip program, reported on it daily. As their lead story most evenings. It had everything. Scandal, corpses, movie stars, mystery, dirt. It was a Made for TV movie in the making.

For instance, Starzy, was in actuality the beneficiary of Jathan's estate. And Robin's too for that matter. It had ended up that among Jathan's papers they found a handwritten —but unwitnessed — will. There being no other relatives for either Jathan, or his brother, to contest it the one page document was sent to probate and accepted by the court.

It was also found that Robin had his own apartment in the same building John Weatherwax had lived in. Upstairs one floor and smaller than John's place it held what few pitiable processions Robin owned. Among them was the original Miro sketch that had been used in his and John's first sting operation. Worth several thousand in its own right it was eventually returned to its rightful owner, Blossom Skyler, out in California. The Chagall that Bevan Jones had purchased was legally hers also, but he was able to broker a deal that allowed him to keep it in his own collection.

With Jathan's will accepted Starzy became the de facto owner of over one-hundred and fifty original paintings by the now very famous artist. Including all his watercolors and sketches. Her being the owner of such substantial works turned out to be a good thing, since the notoriety Starzy garnered from the entire fiasco had put a huge crimp in her movie career. In just the few weeks after the murders she had, reportedly, lost two leading parts in big studio A pictures, received several offers for Z-grade exploitation vehicles, and was looking for new talent representation — her agents had given up handling her. She was "seeking other avenues of expression" as her PR flacks would have it. Not many careers in Hollywood could survive murder charges and the trial that followed. Even Lana Turner's career had suffered from the Johnny Stompanato affair and she wasn't the murderer; at least according to the jury.

Starzy chose to continue the relationship with the Margo Greene Gallery that Jathan — no, it wasn't Jathan, was it? It was Robin who had brokered that deal — Cliff notes would be helpful, huh?

Both Margo and Starzy stood to make a small fortune from the partnership. As long as the publicity kept rolling along Jathan's prices kept rising. Even Len had done some checking — the Jathan drawing he had salvaged from the subway was worth seven or eight thousand dollars already. No telling what a painting would go for with an art market as volatile as it was lately. Just recently a Van Gogh sunflower painting had been auctioned off for almost forty million dollars.

Starzy, as executor of the estate, had Robin's body cremated. Then, along with Jathan's ashes, the cremains were scattered somewhere off the Pacific Coast Highway without ceremony. John Weatherwax's family came to New York and took his body back to his home state for burial in the family plot. JB was a help to them and through his own investigation provided them with some closure by finding out further details about what had happened to him. As payment John's mother presented him with a Hockney sketch her son had owned. Sweets, Weatherwax's dog, was unwanted by any of his relatives, so she had settled in nicely as JB's new pet.

JB did go out with Rex, Bevan Jones' security chief, on one date. One Tuesday night a week after the art show at the Greene Gallery. Dinner and drinks. It went okay, but there was no future in it. Rex's military background had rendered him closed off and uncommunicative, far too stoic for JB's more open sensibilities. Plus a frustrating night spent jockeying for who was going to be top between them killed any chance of more happening.

Bevan Jones finally stopped calling when JB flat out told him he wasn't interested in seeing him again.

He'd probably moved on to someone more compliant and open to his advances. There were plenty of takers JB was sure.

Len had been very busy. His co-star, Lee Arden, had left the show so there were rehearsals with her replacement. She was one more Hollywood has-been looking to make a comeback on Broadway. It was like working with a blob of suet pudding, Len said. The show, he was certain, would not survive the change and would end up closing before his contract ran out. The vicissitudes of the theater. His activities with the gay militants at ACT-UP had increased also. He was attending demonstrations—called zaps by the members—almost weekly now.

In point of fact, Len was attending a zap as this is being written. Something about taking over the lobby of one of the pharmaceutical companies main offices downtown. There was supposed to be a march from Tompkins Square and then a gathering at the front of the building before they crashed the lobby. Len had been almost giddy with anticipation over it.

❊·❊·❊

The phone rang and JB hit the save button on his computer before he went to answer it.

"Oh, JB, its you. I thought I'd get the machine. Anyway, you have got to get yourself down here. Now." Len sounded troubled, with an undercurrent of distraught. In the background JB could hear the confusion of many overlapping voices from a number of people punctuated by the wail of a police siren.

"Where are you, Len? Are you at the rally?"

"Rally isn't the right word, JB. Its more like a panic mob attack here."

"What's going on?"

"You remember that we were going to meet and march to the company offices from the Square?"

"Um-hum."

"Well, that went exactly as we planned. Someone even supplied a prop coffin we could carry with us, symbolizing the many people that have died due to the greediness of the drug companies."

"Yeah. So?"

"And that's what happened. Six men to a side. We all carried that frigging coffin for blocks. Chanting slogans. Making our presence heard. When we got to the building where the company was we found out the front doors were barricaded. Locked. So we couldn't get in. We went ahead with the demonstration anyway. And the planned speeches. Then someone had the bright idea that we should smash in the glass doors with the coffin we'd carried."

"So, you're up to destruction of private property so far."

"The casket was passed to the door over everybody's heads and finally right up to the front. Four guys had hold of it. They swung it back and let it go. The coffin hit the doors and instead of the doors breaking the coffin fell to pieces."

"So you avoided committing the crime?"

"Not necessarily. When the coffin broke open something fell out from inside it."

"What?"

"A body, JB. And not a dummy, a real flesh and blood dead body. Well, as you would guess, that caused a huge panic. You know how a dead body can clear a room. It looked like some blackhole had opened up. I've never seen that many people move so far so fast."

"I can understand why? Who was it?"

"Who was the dead guy?"

"That's right. It was a guy, was it?"

"Not that you would notice. But it turned out it was. Do you remember last May? When we went to the ballet?"

They had indeed gone to the ballet, and taken great delight in juxtaposing the beauty of the dance to the clumping noises the dancers made on the wooden stage. They were draft horses with grace. The ballet they'd attended wasn't a typical company though. Not the New York City Ballet by any means. What they had gone to see was a company of men in drag tutu's doing comedic parodies of traditional ballet scenes. The company had met with near universal acclaim, not only for the comedy dances they presented, but for the technical expertise of the dancers themselves.

"I remember, but what does it have to do with this?"

"Do you remember that they did an excerpt from *Cinderella*? The scene with the wicked stepmother?"

"Yes. Len, I remember. Will you get to the point, please"

"I have. I mean I am. I'm at the point. What I'm saying is the person in the coffin was the dancer who played the part of the evil queen that night. The dead person is Madame Notia Onyalifenskya from the *Ballet de Marrakech du Morocco* dance troupe. That's why you've got to get down here. There's a dead drag queen in a tutu lying in the street."

JB was already getting into his coat when Len was saying dead and dancer.

Here we go again....

About the author:

Ken Lansdowne has lived in California, Nevada, New York City, New Mexico, and now lives in Denver Colorado.

The first novel in *The Bent Mystery* series is *Secrets Don't Belong In Closets*, the beginning. Second is *A Murderous Ball of Fluff*. *The Fairy Dust Killer* is the third. Fourth is *Home Sweet HoMo*. Fifth is *Dance:Ten Murder:Maybe?*. Sixth is *A Mystery, Wrapped In A Mystery, Surrounded By A Mystery.* Seventh is *The Art Of Death,* and number eight is *Bathhouse Bloodbath!*

There is also a Gay themed Christmas novella: *Jacob Marley*

If you would like to get an automatic e-mail when the next book in the series is ready for release sign up at k.lansd@outlook.com. Simply put the word "LIST" in the subject line of your email. Your e-mail address will never be shared and you can unsubscribe at any time.

Word-of-mouth is crucial for any author to succeed. If you enjoyed the book please consider leaving an online review, even if it is only a line or two: it would make all the difference and would be very much appreciated. If you didn't like it I apologize for taking up your time: my purpose was only to entertain or give you a laugh or two.

Made in the USA
Columbia, SC
06 July 2020